"I Like the Way Magnum's Beautiful Representative Conducts Business."

Tracy looked at him; his eyes were filled with desire and passion. She watched a smile, possibly of satisfaction, lift the corners of his mouth. His voice was low; he was thoroughly enjoying himself. The arm that had been holding her against his body slowly relaxed and she slid down so she was no longer on tiptoe.

"Now," he whispered, "I want to know . . ." His hand still moved over her back. "Does Magnum always send beautiful women to con men out of their land? And if so, tell me what special favors you are offering."

ELLEN LANGTRY

says that her first dream was to learn to read, her second to learn to write. Not long after that she began to long to write a book of her own, an ambition she fulfilled recently with the help of Silhouette Books, where we are proud to present her work to you.

Dear Reader:

Silhouette has always tried to give you exactly what you want. When you asked for increased realism, deeper characterization and greater length, we brought you Silhouette Special Editions. When you asked for increased sensuality, we brought you Silhouette Desire. Now you ask for books with the length and depth of Special Editions, the sensuality of Desire, but with something else besides, something that no one else offers. Now we bring you SILHOUETTE INTIMATE MOMENTS, true romance novels, longer than the usual, with all the depth that length requires. More sensuous than the usual, with characters whose maturity matches that sensuality. Books with the ingredient no one else has tapped: excitement.

There is an electricity between two people in love that makes everything they do magic, larger than life—and this is what we bring you in SILHOUETTE INTIMATE MOMENTS. Look for them this May, wherever you buy books.

These books are for the woman who wants more than she has ever had before. These books are for you. As always, we look forward to your comments and suggestions. You can write to me at the address below:

Karen Solem
Editor-in-Chief
Silhouette Books
P.O. Box 769
New York, N.Y. 10019

ELLEN LANGTRY
The Fierce Gentleness

Silhouette Desire
Published by Silhouette Books New York
America's Publisher of Contemporary Romance

SILHOUETTE BOOKS, a Simon & Schuster Division of
GULF & WESTERN CORPORATION
1230 Avenue of the Americas, New York, N.Y. 10020

ISBN: 0-671-46318-7

First Silhouette Books printing May, 1983

10 9 8 7 6 5 4 3 2 1

America's Publisher of Contemporary Romance

Printed in the U.S.A.

To Georgia Bockoven
and
Heidi Evans;
both of you know why. . . .

The Fierce
Gentleness

1

❦❦❦❦❦❦❦❦

Damn the man, where is he?" Tracy Cole muttered, looking across the now empty room toward the tall French doors. No one there, of course.

The young woman nervously pushed back the sleeve of her blue dress to look at a tiny gold watch. The hands had crept slowly from the 10:10 position to 10:17. Marc Durand would be exactly two hours late at 10:30. Then she would leave. No more waiting just fifteen minutes longer, as she had been doing since nine o'clock. At 10:30 she would definitely leave.

Tracy sat in the former solarium, now dining room, of a late-1800s Greek Revival mansion that had been converted to an inn. Plants, potted trees and hanging ferns, the room's only decorations, softened the starkness of the glass and wood walls. Scattered around the dining room were a dozen linen-covered tables, each with a small vase filled with chrysanthemums and sprigs of baby's breath. Two waitresses had already cleared the breakfast dishes and reset the tables for lunch.

Gas heaters helped warm the room, but the heat didn't

9

reach Tracy's feet, and nylons and high heels offered no protection against the cold drafts that chased across the marble floor. Her back ached from sitting on the straight chair; her tense neck muscles signaled a possible headache. The seven-hour drive the day before from Sun Valley, Idaho, over the twisting canyon road had been tiring, and she hadn't slept well in the strange bed. Banging her elbows on the table, Tracy set both cheeks on her fists and sighed impatiently. She wanted to go outside and stroll down to the sparkling river at the end of the garden, to sit on the rock wall and throw stones at the snowcapped boulders.

The day before, the sky had been an empty rice bowl with only thin wispy clouds crackling the azure porcelain glaze, so that morning Tracy had been pleasantly surprised to discover that a snowstorm had come while she slept. The young waitress who had brought the scrambled eggs and bacon glanced out the window and said, "Hard winter coming. Early snow is always a sure sign. It'll be bad for the cattlemen and sheepmen."

But to Tracy, nothing so beautiful could be bad. She looked beyond the snow-covered terrace to an English-style garden, the rosebushes resembling dead sticks poked in cotton. A frosting of snow weighted the branches of the pine trees, pointing their boughs gracefully to the earth. As a backdrop to this Christmas-card scene, a ring of dark, brooding mountains stood sentinel, their craggy spires awash with gold from the morning sun that peeked out for a flashing moment before disappearing again behind gray clouds. After a long and unusually hot autumn in New York, this weather felt delightful.

Turning from the dazzling view, Tracy again checked the entrance for Marcus Durand. Still no sign of him. When she had arrived for her appointment with him, the room had been half full of men—the town's business and civic leaders, Tracy assumed—all wearing similar western-cut suits and cowboy hats. Their covert glances and whispered speculations had amused her. Undoubtedly they wanted to know who she was and why she was here. In a town this size, everyone would soon know that she had come from Magnum Mining to try to buy Marc Durand's wilderness area. What would their reactions be to a cobalt mine near their small town? Friendly or hostile?

When the men had finally filtered out and their laughter no longer reverberated in the glass-walled room, Tracy had forced herself to relax. After four refusals of more coffee, the waitress left her alone in the peaceful silence. The room had no piped-in music, and she was glad; country-western tunes she had listened to in the car would seem strangely out of place in this mansion. Chamber music would be more appropriate.

The night before, when she registered, Mrs. Quartermain, the housekeeper, had given her a brief history of Mille Fleur House.

"Tobias Brewster, Idaho's Silver King, built this as his private residence. But last year, because of inflation and all, the owner, Miss Schell, had the sun room changed to accommodate diners, and the back parlor became a bar." With the last word a tiny shudder shook the woman's thin shoulders, as if the thought of a bar in this stately old house were deplorable to her.

"We rent a few rooms." Her voice became brighter. "But we're really not a public hotel. We like to rent to people we know—visiting salesmen and cattle buyers and such. We're more like a guest house."

Tracy smiled at this dubious distinction and changed the subject. "And Miss Schell is . . . ?"

"Elise Schell. She's a widow—took back her maiden name after her husband, Frank Harlow, died last year. She owns this place now that her grandfather is ailing. They both live on the second floor, in a lovely suite she's

11

decorated with furniture she found in the attic. She's such a clever girl. They've been in Seattle for several days, but they'll be back soon. You'll still be here?"

Hidden in this question, Tracy suspected, was a deep curiosity about herself. "Oh, yes, I'll be here for a few days."

Mrs. Quartermain would have continued talking, but Tracy cut her off, claiming fatigue. Belying her apparent frailness, the woman effortlessly lifted the suitcases and took Tracy to her third-floor room.

"The bathroom's down the hall, dear, and you'll be the only guest on this floor," Mrs. Quartermain explained, after turning back the bedspread. "You just make yourself at home; only the maid or I would come up, so you needn't fear a thing." Tracy was so tired that nothing would have bothered her.

This morning, sitting in the dining room of Mille Fleur House, Tracy thought of Elise and her grandfather, sorry they had gone out of town. Since they were the co-owners of the land she had come here to buy, she wanted to talk to them. They already appeared to favor her plan, but perhaps they could have told her something about Durand before she faced him . . . if she ever got the opportunity.

Ten-twenty. Ten more minutes and she could go to her room and change her clothes. She shouldn't have worn a silk shirtwaist dress here. For this cold dining room, Tracy realized, she would have been better off in her "woman-executive uniform"—a dark blue or brown suit with a skirt, matching jacket and a white blouse with no ruffles to soften the outfit's tailored effect. Not as chic as this dress, perhaps, but definitely warmer.

She glanced at her watch again. Ten-twenty-one. She tried to reason with her growing anger, telling herself that he would surely have a good excuse, maybe an avalanche or a death in the family. But damn it, excuse or not, he could at least have the courtesy to call! She felt like a subaltern kept waiting in a general's anteroom. Unconsciously, she reached toward the small bouquet in the middle of the round table and absently picked the petals off the pale-gold mum. Each almond-shaped segment denoted a known fact about Marcus Aurelius Durand: early thirties; divorced; childless; educated in agribusiness; cattle rancher; shrewd businessman; pilot of his own plane; listed as one of Idaho's numerous millionaires; active in local civic affairs; a poker player of reputed excellence; co-owner of the land that held the rich deposits of cobalt she was here to buy—and, damn it, late!

The petals on the white tablecloth now resembled a pile of miniature autumn leaves; Tracy plucked one more. It stood for Durand's elusiveness. Months of preliminary work had been completed. The geologists had reported that cobalt was here in abundant supply and could be extracted efficiently and inexpensively. All the company needed was Durand. After Tracy had waited weeks for him to answer her numerous phone calls and letters, a succinct telegram had arrived. He would meet with a representative from Magnum Mining on Friday, October 14, 8:30 A.M., at Mille Fleur House, Brewster, Idaho.

Her boss, Jonathan Allen, had insisted that they go to lunch to celebrate this first encouraging sign that Durand might cooperate. He toasted her with champagne. "Here's to Tracy Cole, Magnum's first woman in management. She will blaze a trail so other women can prove to these narrow-minded company officers that women belong on directors' boards—not behind ironing boards."

She grinned at his turn of phrase and lifted her glass to propose a matching toast. "Here's to Jonathan Allen, who held my hand after what happened in Ludlum, California, and who, after I received my Dear Jane letter from Eric Schaeffer, put a bandage on my broken heart."

The arrival of Durand's precipitous summons had helped her forget the painful memories of the last eight months by giving her less than two days to prepare for the trip to Idaho. She felt as if she had been shoved into a cement mixer. Lack of sleep, combined with the rushed flight from New York to Salt Lake City, the bumpy ride in the two-engine prop plane to Sun Valley and the long drive to Brewster, gave her a sense of unreality and disorientation. After her arrival for the appointment that morning she had been taut with anticipation. Now she felt deflated—like a bride left standing at the altar.

A dozen times in the past hour she had started to call him, then talked herself out of it. Having to wait was difficult, but psychologically advantageous. It reshuffled the cards and gave her a better hand. Tracy had come to him; now he had to come to her, cowboy hat dangling from work-stained fingers, an apology on his lips.

This thought helped cool her anger. She sighed and looked at her watch. Ten-twenty-six. Under her nervous fingers, the once lovely chrysanthemum now resembled the last rose of summer. Ashamed of having mutilated its beauty, she rearranged the bouquet so the mum's bald spot wouldn't show. The petals went in her pocket. After folding her napkin back into its original shape she signed the bill and added a generous tip for the patient waitress.

Time to go at last. She pushed back her chair and stood. Her legs tingled from sitting so long. Even though her head felt hot, she was chilled, and intended to go directly to her room for warmer clothes and fur-lined boots. Next time she ate in here she'd wear long johns and mukluks.

As she picked up her briefcase and shoulder bag she heard the sound of heavy footsteps behind her. Sensing that it was the two-hour-late Mr. Durand, Tracy arranged her features in what she hoped was an imperious expression, turned and watched a broad-shouldered man dressed in a plaid shirt, faded blue jeans and boots walk purposefully toward her. As he neared her his smile showed even teeth, startlingly white against his tanned face. Tracy forced herself to remain impassive against his disarmingly friendly grin.

"T. A. Cole?" Surprise flickered in the man's eyes. He put out his hand, taking hers in a firm grip. "Hello. I'm Marc Durand and I'm late."

Tracy noticed that his hands were meticulously clean, destroying the image she had conjured up of Durand as a scruffy cowboy with dirty nails.

"Yes, I know." The words were spoken with a touch of icy anger.

Instead of responding to her curt remark he released her hand and stood relaxed, surveying her with a critical eye. Tracy felt rather like a heifer he was contemplating buying. During the few moments of his thorough inventory Tracy conducted one of her own. His dark curly hair was ruffled, as if the wind had toyed with it. On closer scrutiny his face was not as handsome as she had first thought. She had known better looking men than Marc Durand. He had a slight bump in his nose, cheekbones that were a tad too pronounced, a mouth that was a little too sensuous. Despite these flaws, Tracy had to admit that there was a vitality about him, an attractiveness that hadn't been revealed in the magazine photo she had once seen. When the article had appeared a year ago the picture had showed him with a mustache, frowning at the camera as if he didn't want to be bothered by such nonsense. Now he was cleanshaven and looked younger —less stern and forbidding. He was taller than she had imagined, and his lean frame showed the wiry strength of a man familiar with hard physical labor.

After her gaze had traveled the length of his body she looked up at his face. Against his tanned skin his eyes were a startling blue, the color of cornflowers, and showed his amusement. He had noticed her inspection of him.

"I'm glad you can give as well as receive. I know I like what *I* see." An impish grin crinkled one corner of his mouth. "Do you?"

"Don't be flattered, Mr. Durand. Just a matter of what's sauce for the gander, and all that."

"Point well taken. But let's not inspect each other in this drafty room. You look chilled." He took her briefcase and guided her across the dining room. He smelled of horses and wood smoke, of soap and the tang of fresh air. Tracy breathed in deeply, enjoying the scent. Most men she knew used cologne or aftershave, odors that couldn't compare with this for setting the imagination racing. The thought came as a shock, and she concentrated on keeping up with Marc's long stride. Without slowing down, he asked, "Did you have a tiring trip? I understand you drove from Sun Valley."

"Yes. It took me seven hours. How did you know I drove?"

"Because there are only two ways to get here: drive or fly. Your telegram just said T. A. Cole would meet with me on Friday as I requested." He opened the tall French doors and allowed her to precede him. "You must have come in late or Mrs. Quartermain would have let me know." Out in the hall, they turned left and headed toward the front of the house. "At least you got here before the snow. You should see that pass now."

Tracy shuddered at the thought, remembering the road's tortuous twists and hairpin curves, the sheer cliffs that dropped away to deep canyons.

"Why didn't you fly?"

"I didn't anticipate such a difficult drive. Besides, I wanted to see Idaho. This is my first trip here."

They walked into the spacious foyer, and Marc led her past the curving staircase to a pair of ornate wood sliding doors. They entered and Marc slid the panels closed. Tracy glanced around the room. It looked as if not one thing had been changed since Tobias Brewster drank port and smoked cigars in here. In fact, she could still smell a faint aroma of tobacco that had permeated the dark mahogany paneling. Tracy hurried toward the welcoming fire; she longed to slip off her shoes and thaw her aching feet. After placing her handbag on the floor, she sat in a wing-back chair near the fireplace. She tried to relax and waited for Marc Durand to make the first move.

Marc's earlier comments about her trip seemed to be the extent of his small talk. He said nothing, just hit the logs with a brass poker and threw on more wood, causing sparks to scatter in a frenzied dance.

Finally he sat opposite her in a matching chair, and again his bold gaze roamed over her. "Well, T. A. Cole, you are a surprise." He glanced at her left hand. "I assume it's Miss Cole, or should I say Ms.?"

Ignoring that, Tracy asked, "In what way am I a surprise?"

Marc leaned back and crossed his legs. "I assumed the representative of such a large mining company would be *Mr.* T. A. Cole. What do the initials stand for?"

"Tracy Amanda." She had purposely left off the "Miss" or "Ms." before her name, interested in Marc Durand's reaction when he discovered he would be working with a woman. She had done this before and the results had varied from superciliousness to a seduction attempt. But Marc hadn't overreacted, had easily recovered from his surprise, in fact. So far, so good. "Nowadays, one shouldn't assume that business deals will be conducted only by men. I'm sure you'd discover that fact if you ever ventured out of Idaho."

"You make me sound like a hick who doesn't know about the grand liberation of the female population of America. Is that what you're implying?" He spoke quietly, one eyebrow arched, giving him an amused look.

Instead of responding, Tracy shrugged and stared at the fire. Because Marc had offered no explanation for being late, she had wanted to put him in his place. Perhaps men didn't believe, in apologizing to lowly women in Idaho. What had happened to the Code of the Old West that dictated that women were to be revered and protected? It was probably as dead as chivalry on a New York subway.

The silence dragged on until Marc spoke. "I have a feeling I'm getting a backlash of anger for being late." At his words, Tracy looked over at him. With mocking sincerity, he went on, "I most humbly and sincerely apologize." He placed his hand over his heart in a gesture of abject remorse.

So, Tracy thought, Mr. Marc Durand can be sarcastic.

"I shall explain," he said, his face still overly serious. "I spent most of the night with a lady who had had an accident. So, of course, I had to care for her with all my loving attention and medical knowledge."

"Oh, of course. I understand." All night, fine; but half the morning, too? Tracy kept her thoughts to herself.

"That's why I'm dressed like this." He looked down and picked up a piece of straw from his sleeve. He placed it in the corner of his mouth and returned his gaze to Tracy. "My friend had injured her leg—and a very lovely leg it was, too."

It suddenly hit Tracy. He was teasing her, wanting her to be jealous of his lady of the night. She wasn't that dumb.

"I may be a newcomer out here, but I can tell when I'm having my leg pulled, if you'll pardon the expression. You had to spend the night with a sick friend, and a man's best friend is his horse. Right?"

"Well, well, the lady is both beautiful and smart. My lucky day." Marc made a little bow to her and continued speaking. "I did try to call, but the storm downed a line. We *are* on the outer fringes of civilization, you know, and have far fewer amenities than a big city."

Marc shifted in his chair, removed the straw from his mouth and twirled it, the light from the fire making it resemble a thin stick of gold. He waited for her next remark without looking at her. Tracy studied his face again and decided she had better change tactics. Bantering with him placed her in a no-win situation, and sarcasm could get out of hand. Besides, he had apologized and now the ball was in her court.

"I most humbly and sincerely accept your apology." Tracy's hand went to her heart, mimicking Marc's gesture. Then she smiled and said, "I was irritable because I was cold. The floor of that room is so frigid I'm surprised they didn't make a skating rink out of it."

"You should have waited in your room. I would have found you." His deep voice took on a seductive quality; there was an unmistakable meaning in his words. He leaned forward, placing his arms on his knees. The light from the fire touched his hair, highlighting the black curls with gold. He looked as if he wanted to say something more, but then his manner changed. He leaned back in the chair and said, "I told Elise when she chose the solarium for a dining room that it would be cold enough to freeze the . . ." He paused and reworded his sentence. "I mean, it would be cold in winter despite the gas heaters. Have you thawed out?"

"Yes, thanks." She looked around for the briefcase

that Marc had carried for her. "We should get started. I'll need my case. The papers are in it." Tracy glanced around the room.

Marc stood, but instead of locating the briefcase he walked to the fireplace and noisily revived the fire. "Let's not talk business now. I'm going to order breakfast." He moved to the side of the mantel, reached out and picked up a round disk about the size of a doughnut. A cord on one end was attached to the wall. Tracy had seen one in her room, but assumed it no longer worked. She'd have to call for room service sometime.

Turning a crank near a square of metal mesh, Marc looked at Tracy. "Want anything?"

From the small screen on the wall Tracy heard a buzz, and then a woman shouted, "Hello? Who's there?"

Before answering, Marc waited for Tracy to speak. "Tea, please."

"Right." He placed the antique microphone to his mouth and said, "Hello, Vivian? This is Marc Durand." He stopped talking while the disembodied voice asked how he was doing. "I'm fine, Vivian, but hungry. Could you bring me some breakfast? Whatever you've got, coffee, a pot of tea and two cups. I'm in the sitting room off the main hall."

"Be about ten minutes, Marc." A click abruptly ended the conversation.

"That's a clever invention. I wonder if it'll catch on."

Marc sat down again and smiled. "It only works if someone's in the kitchen to receive the call. As a kid I used to come to this house to play with Elise and Kent Regan and Frank Harlow. . . ." His voice trailed off, lost in memories. "We about drove Mrs. Schell and the housekeeper crazy using that speaker." He laughed, then became serious and sighed, a sound that strangely affected Tracy, making her want to comfort him for some reason.

Seeming to shake himself free of the past, he asked, "Tell me, how did you become a representative for Magnum Mining?"

Tracy stared at the fire for a moment, conjuring up her own memories. "There's not much to tell, really. I graduated from Northwestern University with a degree in business administration and public relations. Then I got my MBA at Harvard Business School and was hired by a Magnum recruiter the week before graduation. I've been there ever since." The simple words could never convey the hard work and dedication it had taken to reach a position where top companies vied for her services, where she could pick and choose the best deal.

"Do you like your job?" Marc sounded genuinely interested, not just polite.

"Love it. Magnum is a good growth company with a new president who made a lot of changes in a tradition-bound family firm. I was the first woman in their executive-training program. Since I started three years ago, two more women have been hired. I helped choose them." Despite her attempt to subdue it, a hint of pride was in her voice.

"You've taken no geology or mining engineering or even advanced sand, pebble and rock study?"

Was he patronizing her? His face showed only interest. She shook her head. "I deal with the public, negotiating sales, calming the townspeople's fears about a mining company coming to their area, that sort of thing. I've learned a great deal about mining though and can read, understand and even interpret for a layman the data in a geologist's report. An MBA is very adaptable." There. If he had been patronizing her, she chalked one up for her side.

For the first time since she had met Marc Durand, she was at ease, enjoying the game they were playing. While she talked he had sat quietly, rarely taking his eyes off her face. Nothing showed in his expression to reveal what he was thinking.

"Tell me about yourself and your ranch," Tracy asked, stretching her feet closer to the fire. Marc's gaze traveled up and down her long legs, and he smiled appreciatively. She refrained from pulling them back; let him look if he wants. She said, "I saw that article about you last year. You certainly don't look like that picture. You were scowling."

"I didn't want to do that article or have my picture taken. To tell you the truth, I never even saw it after it was printed. Too embarrassed. I took a lot of teasing about that."

Tracy was about to ask why he had agreed to be interviewed when she heard a knock. Marc hurried over to open the doors.

"Ah, Vivian, what service."

"The breakfast crew's left, and you've thrown my lunch schedule off." She glanced at Tracy and smiled, saying, "Miss Cole. I heard you were staying here. I'm Vivian, the cook."

"Hello, Vivian. You're terrific. Those croissants were the best I've ever tasted."

A pleased smile creased the heavy woman's features as she set the tray on the table. "Thanks, miss, glad you liked them. See you two later."

Marc walked Vivian to the door, his arm around her shoulders as he whispered in her ear and kissed her cheek. She shut the door, and Tracy could hear her laughter floating down the hall. Marc pulled two chairs up to the table. While Tracy poured her tea from a fragile-looking Haviland pot into a matching cup, Marc began to eat.

"God, I was hungry. Want some?" he mumbled between bites.

Before she could say no, Marc held out a buttered croissant with strawberry jam. Tracy couldn't resist.

"Thanks. I'd like to steal Vivian. She's fantastic." Tracy licked her fingers.

"Don't you dare entice Vivian away. I eat here every time I come to town. She's the only thing that keeps me from complete malnutrition."

Tracy looked at Marc's excellent physical condition. Malnutrition or obesity would never be problems for him.

"You mean that in all this vast area there's no woman besides Vivian who would cook for a hungry bachelor like you? I find that a little hard to believe." Tracy said the words with humor, but was very interested in what his answer would be. She knew he was divorced; why had he never remarried? Five years was a long time.

"Oh, there are plenty of women around here, but no one cooks like Vivian. When I was a constantly hungry sixteen, I asked her to be my wife. You know, I think she was tempted. Sure took her a long time to say no."

"It must have been your modesty."

Marc wiped his mouth with a linen napkin to hide a smile. "Could be," he said with a straight face. "Want the job?"

"I don't cook."

"Pity," he said.

While Marc continued to eat, he told her some of the early history of Idaho. Few people knew, he said, that during the 1890s union troubles with miners had led to the assassination of a former governor. Tracy had already acquainted herself with Idaho's wealth-producing and sometimes violent mining operations. Called the Gem State, it had produced millions of dollars worth of silver and gold. But the cost in human endeavor had been high. Tracy wondered if Idaho's past would prejudice this man against considering the sale of his land.

Between sentences Marc would hand Tracy a piece of bacon, a segment of orange, another piece of croissant. The intimacy of these acts heightened Tracy's awareness of him. Even though his language was neutral, when his hand brushed hers or their gazes met, he conveyed a sensually erotic message that changed the simple act of sharing food into an act of love. The message he transmitted bypassed Tracy's mind and was received by her physical being. She felt her heartbeat quicken; her breath came in through a constricted throat; her body ached with newly awakened need.

Confused, she looked down, picked up her cup with trembling hands and blew on the hot liquid. Through lowered lashes she observed Marc over the rim. What would it be like to sit across from this man the morning after spending a night with him? What would they talk about? How would she feel after those strong hands had caressed her or those lips had kissed her? The thought brought a blush to her cheeks. She set the cup down, and it clattered in the saucer. Pouring herself more tea, Tracy tried to concentrate on something else. But the questions perversely continued spinning in her mind. How many nights did he spend alone? Probably very few, she answered herself. No virile bachelor of thirty-two who looked like Marc Durand would have to climb under the blankets without some woman eagerly waiting for him. Before she could stop herself, the picture that formed behind her half-closed lids was one of Tracy Cole lying there, her arms outstretched toward Marc, reaching for him. . . .

The sound of Marc's voice broke into her thoughts, but she couldn't decipher what he said. "Pardon? I didn't hear you."

"Because you weren't listening," he admonished. Then his voice changed, again taking on that low seductive tone. "What were you thinking?" He leaned over the table, staring at her face intently.

Tracy was flustered by Marc's probing gaze and quickly decided that the best defense was a good offense. "As soon as you're finished eating, we should begin going over the . . ."

Tracy never finished her sentence. Without her knowing how it happened, Marc was standing before her, pulling her to her feet.

"I can read a woman's eyes, and you were definitely not thinking about Magnum." Tracy tried to step away, startled speechless by Marc's quick actions. "I saw longing and desire in those lovely eyes of yours." Tracy shook her head in denial, unable to find the words.

"Oh, yes, I did, and I'm going to work very hard to keep that dreamy, wanting-to-be-satiated look on your face."

Marc spread one hand across her back, pressing her against him. His other hand came up to the back of her head, entangling itself in her long hair. Just as Tracy opened her mouth to protest Marc's lips gently touched hers. Tracy's palms were flat against his chest and through his shirt she could feel his heart beating beneath her hand. Then the kiss changed; he claimed her lips as if he wanted to devour them. His arms tightened, and he held her with an insistent pressure that molded her body to his in a way that left no doubt about what he was experiencing.

Her well-planned method of presenting Magnum's proposal was being more thoroughly destroyed every moment she stood there in his arms, letting his kiss deepen, responding to the way his hands moved over her back, past her waist, down to her hips and beyond, where he grasped her closer to him.

Marc's tongue tentatively touched hers, and new sensations erupted in Tracy with an intensity that shook her. She tried to pull away, but it was too late. Marc wasn't about to lose the advantage he had gained. He demanded and got responses from her that she would never have believed possible. Long moments passed, and finally Marc raised his head. When Tracy looked at him his eyes were filled with desire and passion. She watched a smile of satisfaction lift the corners of his mouth.

"I like the way Magnum's beautiful representative conducts business." Marc's voice was low; he was thoroughly enjoying himself. The arm that had been holding her against his body slowly relaxed, and she slid down so that her feet were once again flat on the floor.

"Now," he whispered, "I want to know . . ." His hand still moved over her back. ". . . does Magnum always send beautiful women to con men out of their land? And if so, tell me what special favors you're offering."

2

~~~~~~~~~~~~~

The words hit Tracy as if she had been physically struck. A chill tingled down her spine, and she gasped aloud and stepped back. Marc didn't stop her, letting his arms fall to his sides. They stood face to face like two cats, each waiting for the other to make a move.

A dozen replies came to Tracy's mind, only to be discarded. Finally she spoke, her voice barely audible. "Marc Durand, that is a vile thing to say to a woman." She waited to see if he would speak, but he continued to stand there, looking at her, a frown replacing his smile.

At least now Tracy knew what Marc Durand's position was. His words and actions had clearly spelled out his opinion of her. He had correctly read her thoughts and had seized the opportunity by kissing her. She had responded to those kisses, proving, in his mind, that his assumption had been correct. She had to be crazy. Or perhaps the trip the day before had been more exhausting than she had realized. Or perhaps . . . No, there were no excuses for her behavior. He had kissed her, and she had matched his passion, had thoroughly enjoyed every second of it. But regardless of how pleasurable it was to be held in his arms, she had to erase the impression he had of her, had to reestablish her position, had to make him see her as a professional. Easier said than done.

Tracy took a deep breath and said, "You're all wrong, Mr. Durand. But regardless of your low opinion of me, you had better accept the fact that I'm the company representative and I'm here to see if you and Magnum can come to an amicable agreement concerning the sale of your land." They stood facing each other like adversaries in a ring waiting for the bell. Tracy spoke again. "The company assumed that since you sent for a representative to come here, you were willing to discuss the matter."

She continued to stare unwaveringly at him, her face as unreadable as his. "If we misinterpreted your message about wanting to hear Magnum's deal, I'm sorry."

Marc hardly moved, though a half smile erased his frown. Could he be testing her, wanting her to explode? Determined not to give him the satisfaction, she decided to end this meeting now.

"So . . ." She walked to her chair and found her handbag. ". . . since our initial contact has ended so unpleasantly, perhaps we could meet later, when you have decided whether or not you want to discuss Magnum's proposal. But if you *do* want to hear it, you'll have to deal with *me*."

Without waiting for him to reply, Tracy strode toward the tall sliding doors, her back straight and her steps unhurried. After shoving the doors open she turned and said, "Also, Magnum does *not* dictate what favors I offer. *I* do that. And I have very discriminating taste." She walked away, her footsteps clicking on the floor, matching the staccato rhythm that pounded in her head.

By the time she reached her bedroom her thoughts were full of kaleidoscopic images, dominated by Marc

Durand's sardonically grinning face. Tracy set her bag on a chair and walked directly to the window. She pulled aside the heavy drape and wiped moisture off the glass. As she looked out blindly, all the "should-have-saids" flitted through her mind. She should have said . . . Oh hell, what was the use?

The veil of anger dissipated, and she focused on the downy snowflakes that floated before her eyes. Against the white background, each flake seemed a subtle shade of gray.

She could see the semicircular driveway in front of the mansion. In a few seconds Marc, carrying a heavy jacket, strode toward a pickup truck, got in and slammed the door.

The falling snow softened colors to pastels and made his red truck look ethereal. As he drove past the front of the building he looked up at her window, but made no acknowledgment that he saw her.

"Damn you, Marc Durand," she whispered to the retreating truck, wishing he could hear her.

As she moved away from the window Tracy reached up to unbutton the front of her dress, stepped out of it and carefully hung it in the free-standing fruitwood wardrobe. Unless Durand called to make another appointment she had nothing to do until she could leave. Tired, emotionally drained and feeling cold again, she looked at the canopied bed with its warm blankets and shrugged away her guilt about returning to bed at noon. Pulling back the hand-embroidered bedspread, she lay down on the soft mattress. The white linen coverlet enfolded her in a cocoon of warmth, and she closed her eyes.

Then the ramifications of his words hit her. Would Durand be so prejudiced against working with a woman that he would call off the negotiations? Or would he see her only as a desirable woman and refuse to take her seriously? She tried to assure herself that he wouldn't be so narrow-minded when an old fear returned. After what had happened in Ludlum, losing this deal would probably result in what the company delicately called a reappraisal of her worth to them. How could she ever explain a defeat in Brewster?

In Ludlum she had never really been given the opportunity to show her capabilities. Her failure there had been mostly bad luck. After weeks of exploration and planning, and after having obtained the preliminary impact studies to meet the stringent state and federal requirements, Tracy had gone to Ludlum, California, to finalize the contract with Farnsworth and Bishop, the two owners of the grazing land in question. But they had continually delayed the negotiations, then sold out to another mining company.

Her experience in Ludlum had shaken her belief in her abilities; the forceful words she had said to Marc Durand that morning now sounded hollow and untrue. Perhaps she should have taken her parents' advice and followed the path of so many of her friends: college, teaching, husband, home, children, country club, do-gooder activities. Perhaps she had been wrong in choosing the route that had led a naive twenty-three-year-old to a job at Magnum. But right or wrong, she had committed herself to her career, and by letting nothing distract her, by directing all her energies to the goals that she had set for herself, she had started the slow climb up the corporate ladder. Now, three years later, she made a good salary, rented a small but charming apartment near Central Park and enjoyed numerous social and cultural evenings with friends, both male and female.

Her life was full and satisfying—except for the disappointments of failing at Ludlum and the end of her relationship with Eric Schaeffer.

She and Eric had met at Magnum and had known

each other for a year when he proposed marriage. Then Tracy discovered that Eric assumed that she would quit Magnum after their marriage so she could join him on his long overseas assignments, and a tiny wedge was driven between them. By the time Magnum asked Eric to go to South America for five years, the crack had grown into a chasm. Tracy tried to straddle that widening canyon, a balancing act that had left her emotionally exhausted. When the letter from the jungles of Guyana arrived, typically scribbled on the back of an engineering drawing, she had experienced a feeling of near relief. The decision, Eric said, was up to her: a career with Magnum in New York or marriage to him, moving wherever he was assigned and, if she insisted on working, finding whatever jobs she could.

She couldn't agree to his terms and resolved never to be placed in a position of having to choose between love and her career again. The two *weren't* mutually exclusive, but if she never found a man who agreed—so be it.

Tracy filled her life with activity, and when she thought of Eric, she knew she had made the right decision in remaining at Magnum. Yet sometimes, like forks of summer lightning that disappeared before being seen, flashes of discontent disturbed her sleep. She would awaken and wonder if she were truly happy or merely putting on a good act. By morning those little storms would have passed and she would once again face the day with enthusiasm.

Now, here in Brewster, Idaho, on this snowy afternoon, Tracy lay in her too-soft bed and stared at the white canopy overhead, deciding she had had enough memories. After throwing back the coverlet, she jumped out of bed, walked to the mirror, thought about the disappointing morning and knew it had served to add another item to her list of information about Marc Durand. Perhaps it would help her choose the best method of approach—if he called. Meanwhile, she'd try not to think about Marc Durand at all.

Outside her window, large feathery flakes still drifted down. Not sure if her rental car had snow tires, she decided to walk the few blocks to the center of town. She dressed in warm clothes and fur-lined boots, grabbed her jacket, dashed out of the room and ran to the stairs. As she walked down to the front hall she noticed that the house was immaculately clean, but she remembered a few telltale signs of disrepair, as if money were being spent on essentials and not on replacing worn carpets and upholstery.

Tracy hurried outside, where large snowflakes landed on her light auburn hair and brushed whispery kisses on her cheeks. One dropped into her eye and instantly melted. Walking down the sidewalk, which was lined with enormous cottonwood trees, Tracy admired the expansive lawns and large homes. Their spacious front porches reminded her of her grandmother's house in St. Louis. People cleaning the snow off their sidewalks greeted her with friendliness, and she dodged a snowball thrown by a grinning boy with cheeks the color of apples.

As Tracy walked up the hill toward the main part of town, a feeling of unreality set in, a sensation of having entered another land, another time. The nearer she got to the town square, the more she began to suspect that she was *not* in a typical Idaho town.

When she arrived at the hub of the street, her suspicions were confirmed. This wasn't Idaho, this was a New England village of 100 years ago. A white-steepled church, a staid city hall with BEDFORD COUNTY carved in the granite front and a cut-stone library stood on three corners of the square. All the adjacent buildings were built in the ornate architecture of Victorian times.

Tracy walked through the plaza, following a path trimmed with still-blooming chrysanthemums, the snow making their blossoms droop sadly. Scattered around the empty bandstand were huge leafless poplar and elm trees and lacy ironwork benches. Tracy brushed one off and sat down, trying to comprehend this delightful mélange that blended the mellowed charm of an eastern town with the wild mountains of Idaho.

Looking at the town square, Tracy kept turning to stare at the towering peaks that surrounded the valley. In the failing light of late afternoon, a slight breeze made the snow swirl and turned the scene into a surrealistic collage of muted images. Tracy shook her head in wonder. How had the town been built? How had they got the supplies over the mountains and through the canyon, a trip that had taken her hours in a fast car? Why had it never become a tourist area or a resort for the rich? She was glad that no one had developed it, that it had been left in such a perfect state.

It took a moment for the incongruity of that last thought to occur to her. If Magnum started a cobalt mine near here, this town would never be the same. She knew what happened when a large-scale mining operation came to an area . . . instant blight. Visualizing the large prefab office and house trailers that would be brought in, the fast-food places that would erupt like sores on the face of the town, the noisy, smelly trucks that would carry the ore to a smoke-spewing smelter, Tracy shuddered.

Before she had always justified this aspect of her job, explaining to herself that the nation needed rare and vital minerals like cobalt to free itself from dependence on foreign sources. But now she was faced with a dilemma— a dilemma she wondered if she could solve.

3

~~~~~~~~~~~~~~~

Two hours later, a chilled and confused Tracy returned to Mille Fleur House and immediately filled the tub that sat regally in the oversize bathroom located down the hall from her bedroom. As she stepped in she noticed the blood-red polished nails of the tub's clawed feet. Some fanciful girl had taken the time to manicure the iron paws. Elise Schell?

Smiling, she leaned back and watched the undulating water swirl around her body. Bubbles tickled her chin, and if she moved too fast they threatened to spill onto the floor.

Her walk had eased the painful memories of the past and of Marc Durand, at least temporarily. Now, lying in this luxurious bath, she felt the tensions of the day dissolve completely.

Tracy's stomach rumbled, a reminder that she hadn't had lunch. She'd better hurry or she'd miss dinner, too. Regretfully she finished her bath and stepped out. She toweled herself dry, shivering despite the steamy warmth of the room. Then she slipped into an apricot robe and walked to the pedestal washstand. Its brass faucets looked like gold, and under the glaze of the porcelain bowl were hand-painted flowers and leaves.

Tracy brushed her hair until an aura of copper encircled her face. After a last check around the room, she walked down the hall. The only sound was the slapping of her slippers on the carpet, and she hurried toward the rectangle of light coming from her bedroom. She had left the door open on purpose. The room had seemed stuffy after the fresh air outside, and since she was the only one on the floor, she felt safe.

Once inside, she locked the door and unthinkingly slipped the key into her pocket. The sun had set and the room was dim, so she walked to the table near the unlit fireplace and lit the lamp. Revealed in the pool of light was a large Boston fern sitting in the chair. Wrapped around its white pot were two plaid-shirted arms; jutting out from under it were two denim-covered legs.

Without thinking, she reached over and parted the fronds of the fern to find Marc Durand.

"What are you doing here?" she asked, her voice filled with relief.

"You certainly are trusting to leave your door open and then, without a scream, casually examine your intruder."

"I'm not the hysterical type, and I recognized your shirt." He looked so funny sitting there, like an animated potted palm. Despite herself, Tracy smiled. She released the lacy leaves of the plant, and the fern again obscured his face. Walking toward the bed, she felt shaky, her heart beating like a bird caught in a net. With Marc in the room, she was again reminded of his expert, exciting kisses and his humiliating words. How could she make him forget her passionate response to his lovemaking? How could she repair the damage and begin to establish a working relationship with him?

Marc stood and placed the ceramic pot on the hearth.

Tracy realized that she had seen that fern before. That morning it has been in a white wrought-iron stand in the dining room.

"I didn't know that stealing was among your list of crimes, Mr. Durand."

He turned and smiled, a gesture that changed his face drastically. "I may have many faults, Tracy Cole, possibly including petty theft, but boorishness isn't generally one of them. I came to apologize—not for the kiss, which I thoroughly enjoyed, but for my thoughtless remarks." He sounded genuinely sorry, and Tracy found herself forgiving him without a qualm.

"I needed a token of my contrition, and this was the only thing I could find on such short notice. Long-stemmed roses are hard to get out here in the boonies. Besides, you left your briefcase downstairs, and I thought I'd better return it to you."

He walked toward her, a gleam in his eye that made him look rakishly appealing. Suddenly Tracy was aware of her vulnerability, of how her robe emphasized her breasts, which rose and fell more rapidly with each passing second. But she didn't move away from his scrutiny, refusing to let him know how he disconcerted her.

"I accept your apology, Mr. Durand, and your token of sincerity, as long as Mrs. Quartermain doesn't mind." His nearness was causing her heart to beat in a strange, erratic way. He was looking at her the same way he had that morning, just before he had kissed her.

"Perhaps we could meet for breakfast in the morning?" she asked. She stepped back and moved around him, walking toward the door. "There will be time then for you to read and study Magnum's proposal."

Marc followed her to the door, and she found herself wishing that he wouldn't stand so close. She moved back slightly, but he followed, as if attached to her with strings.

"Tracy Cole." He bent his head down near her ear and breathed deeply. "You smell like a rose garden on a summer's eve. I wonder if you know how entrancing you look, fresh from the bath, all warm and clean." He reached out and fondled the curls at her neck. "Your hair is still damp. . . ."

His touch sent a shiver through Tracy, a reaction that disturbed her. Why, her mind pleaded, should this stranger make her feel this way? She must not let her physical attraction for him destroy her resolve to keep their relationship purely business.

With this thought she said, "Look, I hate to sound like a prude, but I wish you would leave." As she spoke, she turned the doorknob, but nothing happened. Then she remembered that she had locked it; the key was in the pocket of her robe.

Before she could reach for it he moved even closer and leaned his hand against the wall. Tracy's back was against the door now, her own hand caught behind her. She knew that this awkward stance emphasized her breasts, but she didn't dare look down to see how much was revealed. Instead she stared into his eyes, feeling like a trapped rabbit and hoping she didn't resemble one.

"Tracy." He whispered the name, his voice husky with emotion. "How would you like to go . . ." He paused and smiled slowly. She had her mouth open to say a vehement no when he continued, ". . . dancing?"

"Dancing?" She said it aloud, astonished at the innocent word. Before she could stop herself she said, "Square?"

He laughed. "You must think we're terribly provincial out here in the sagebrush. No, I don't mean square dancing. Dancing, like this." Before she could do anything he grabbed her around the waist, reached behind her for her other arm and twirled her around the room, humming a rich baritone rendition of a popular love song.

The suddenness of the action took Tracy completely by surprise, and before she knew it she was following him as if they had danced together for years. They swirled around the bed, to the fireplace and back to the bed. Then her slipper caught on the rug and she fell against him. He lost his balance, too, and they tumbled onto the soft mattress, laughing.

She was on top of him, and before she could untangle the robe from her legs so she could slip off the bed, he had pulled her up so her mouth was directly above his. He placed both hands on the sides of her head, his fingers shoved into her hair. As Tracy began to pull away, he lowered her mouth to his waiting lips.

Tracy's body was stretched out along the full length of his; in this seductive position she didn't dare squirm too strenuously to get away. As soon as he released her mouth she would coldly request that he release her. But her desire to be set free became weaker as Marc's kiss deepened. His hands moved down to her body, and Tracy opened her mouth as their tongues began a dance of their own. As if her body were a separate entity, acting without her knowledge, she began to relax more and more. His hands roamed down her back, over her hips and back up again. She experienced a pleasure she had denied herself for a long time—the intense rapture of having a man communicate his desire for her. Her mind ceased functioning rationally; now it registered only emotions, sensations she had kept buried. The sweet warmth that had begun at her mouth now spread wherever his whisper-soft kisses landed. She could feel his heart racing, the beat matching the thundering rhythm of her own. The heat inside her spread, first to her fingertips, which stroked the skin of his tanned neck. Then the warmth spread down to her breasts, which seemed to have grown fuller and more sensitive, as if waiting for him to cup them. More rapidly now, the fire flowed down and she could feel a throbbing pulse that made her gasp. Marc paused in his exploratory kisses; she pulled away and focused on his deep-blue eyes.

A smile flickered across his face, and he took a long, shaky breath to say, "Welcome to Idaho, Tracy Cole." Reaching up with one hand, he gently pushed her head back down.

As if a switch had clicked on in her brain Tracy became aware of what she was doing. Determined to end this before it went any further, she pulled away from his eager mouth. "Let me go," she whispered and began to struggle. She soon realized her movements were fanning the flame of passion in Marc's eyes. A look of panic must have shown on her face, because the next thing she knew, he had released her and his arms were lying innocently beside him. Too embarrassed to glance again at his face, Tracy looked at the wall as she rolled over and jumped off the bed, straightening her robe and shoving her hair out of her eyes.

Still lying on the bed, he propped his head up with his arm and looked over at her. "Does this mean dancing is out?"

Despite herself, she laughed. He sounded so forlorn, almost as if someone had said he couldn't go to the circus. He jumped up, accepting her laughter as acquiescence. "Good." His quick movement startled her. "We'll eat first. Wear that sexy blue dress you had on this morning. I'll be back in half an hour."

By this time he was at the door, trying to open it. He turned and looked quizzically at her. "Not taking any chances, are you?"

"Oh, get out of here, Marc Durand." She threw the key at him, trying unsuccessfully to look stern.

He easily caught the key in midair. Opening the door,

he paused and turned. "Oh, yes . . . not one word about Magnum or cobalt tonight. See you in half an hour." Before she could protest he was gone.

An exciting vibrancy left with him, which made the room seem disturbingly empty. Tracy walked to the bed and leaned against the tall canopy post. What should she do? Stay in the room? Get dressed and go downstairs to eat? With him or alone?

Suddenly remembering how alive she had felt when he kissed her, she knew she wanted to be with him. Keeping a businesslike attitude would undoubtedly be difficult, but she could do it. Besides, she might learn something more about him and add another piece to the mosaic of his personality.

She opened the wardrobe and searched through her clothes, thinking she'd be damned before she'd wear the blue dress, wanting something warmer for the Arctic Dining Room. After choosing a long, soft wool skirt and coral silk blouse, she dressed with an efficiency born in one who liked to sleep until the very last minute. As she lightly applied her makeup she blushed, remembering how her lips had responded to his. She reminded herself to be careful, to remain neutral toward him. In the past she had had a great deal of practice fending off men's attentions, but Marc operated differently from any other man she had ever sparred with.

Assuring herself that she could handle any situation, she grabbed the off-white shawl that matched the skirt, turned out the lights and slowly walked down the curved staircase. Her fingertips brushing the banister, Tracy felt elegant and regal. Marc waited below, and she watched his eyes follow her descent. She felt a new surge of confidence in herself and her ability to deal with Marcus Aurelius Durand.

When she neared the bottom he reached out his hand

to help her down the last steps. He now wore an open-collar checked shirt covered by a V-neck sweater and tucked into charcoal-gray slacks. Instead of heavy cowboy boots, he had on black loafers.

"Where's your coat?"

"I didn't think I'd need it. We're eating here, aren't we?" Tracy noted that Marc had no jacket.

His gaze roamed from her hair down to her heels, taking in the details of her appearance. She wondered if he noticed that she hadn't worn the blue dress.

"No, we aren't," he said. "You don't really need a coat, though. The car is warm and we don't have far to go."

He took her arm and escorted her outside. The cold hit Tracy and she shivered. Marc seemed attuned to her discomfort and before she knew what he was doing he effortlessly lifted her in his arms and carried her down the snow-covered steps to his car. Once she was in his arms again her nascent confidence in her ability to handle any situation began to ebb.

Marc bent down to open the door, and Tracy could feel the muscles in his arms. This cattle rancher didn't sit around and let others do the hard work necessary to make a ranch successful. His strength and vitality affected her in a strange new way; she blushed at the thoughts that raced through her mind.

As he placed her in the seat he leaned in and lightly kissed her, running his tongue across her mouth, tasting its sweetness, nibbling at her bottom lip. As if aware that Tracy was about to protest, he stood and said, "Just an hors d'oeuvre. My favorite kind."

While he walked around to the driver's side Tracy said a silent "damn" and vowed not to leave herself so open to his advances again.

The red pickup truck had been replaced by an old

41

Buick station wagon with wood-paneled sides. The motor roared into life and settled down to a low purr as they drove down the hill away from the mansion. In the dim light Tracy could see the fine-grained woods of the dashboard. From her brother she had picked up an admiration for old, carefully preserved cars, and she knew how much loving attention it took to care for them. If he had done the work himself, this was another aspect of Marc Durand's personality that surprised her.

"Is this an old family car, or did you buy it?"

"Old family car. My father believed in getting his money's worth. He recycled cars, trucks, ranch equipment. We've got a 1935 tractor we still use around the yard." Now they were traveling on the outskirts of town. Set among deep tracts of pine were farmhouses, their lights looking warm and inviting. The road followed the twistings of the river; Tracy caught occasional glimpses of its tumbling waters.

"For special occasions I bring out the Buick. Idaho winters and bad roads are hard on cars. We use pickup trucks and planes more often."

Remembering his excuse of the morning, she asked, "Don't you occasionally ride long-legged ladies who demand your attention all night?"

After she said the words the double meaning hit her and she stared straight ahead, suddenly embarrassed.

Marc laughed. "I'm not going to comment on that, so stop blushing."

To hide her chagrin Tracy asked, "Where are we going? Does Brewster have a secret nightclub?" Her undercurrent of laughter brought a smile to Marc's face.

"You'll see." He said nothing more, just drove expertly through the quiet night.

A few minutes later he pulled off the road onto a graveled area and stopped the motor. Tracy peeked out and saw a two-story wood-frame building that, except for a porch light, looked dark. It resembled an old house, not a restaurant, and Tracy's confusion intensified.

Marc got out of the car, walked around and again lifted her in his arms to carry her to the front porch. "Next time," she smiled, "I'll wear boots so you won't have to carry me everywhere."

"I don't mind," he said. "As long as there is a next time." He nestled his face in her hair. On the landing he released her knees so she swung to the floor. Keeping an arm around her shoulders, he pushed open the door without knocking and called out, "Maria? We're here."

The first thing that hit Tracy was the indescribable aroma of food. She tried to identify it: tomatoes, herbs and spices, lamb, fresh-baked bread. Her mouth watered, and she felt lightheaded with hunger. She must remember, in this weather and altitude, not to skip meals.

"Ah, Señor Durand." The deep, musically accented voice preceded the woman whose broad bosom was covered by a spotlessly clean apron. "I am pleased to see you again."

"Tracy, this is Señora Valcarlos. Maria, this is Tracy Cole, from New York."

"Señorita Cole, welcome to my home." She reached out, her hand touching Tracy's cheek in a gesture of tenderness and concern. "Come to the fire, you are cold wearing only that shawl. You must learn to dress for this country."

They followed her into a small, comfortable, simply decorated room dominated by a large fireplace with a crackling fire. Tracy walked over to it, rubbing her arms to absorb the heat. While waiting for Marc to finish talking to their hostess, Tracy looked around the room. The eight tables were covered with checkered tablecloths; each held a flickering candle. On one wall were family photographs, the old-fashioned kind where the people looked stiff and self-conscious in ill-fitting clothes. Another wall held a deer head, its baleful eyes staring at her. Under the luckless head were a black-lace fan and a multicolored embroidered shawl.

Tracy hadn't noticed that Marc had approached her until he touched her arm. "Come, sit here." He pointed to a table near the fireplace. Holding a chair out for her, he spoke in a low voice. "Señora Valcarlos is Basque. Have you ever had Basque food before?"

"No, but I like lamb. Isn't that the main ingredient?"

"Yes, lamb and lots of onions, garlic and hot peppers." After sitting down across from her he poured deep red wine into goblets and raised his glass in a salute. "Tracy Amanda Cole, you may not believe this, but I'm glad you've come to Brewster." Without taking his eyes off her, he drank deeply.

His toast surprised and heartened Tracy. Perhaps, just perhaps, she could be successful here. "Thank you. I'm glad—"

Before she could finish the sentence an incredibly handsome young man entered the room. He looked about twenty and had the dark, smoldering good looks of his Spanish and Basque heritage. He greeted Marc and was introduced as Maria's son, Roberto. While he answered Marc's questions about school he kept turning his large brown eyes in Tracy's direction, then glancing away in embarrassment.

"Will you play for us later, Rob?"

"Oh, yes, I would love to. I have a new twelve-string guitar, and I can make it sing like a choir of angels." As he talked about music, he lost his bashful look.

The señora entered, carrying a tray laden with a tureen of steaming soup and a basket of sourdough bread.

"Roberto, help me set these dishes down. You were talking about your guitar again, weren't you?"

44

"Sí, Mama; may I play for the señor and señorita later, when I get my work finished?"

The large woman looked at her son with love. "If they desire it." To Marc she said, "When you are finished with the soup, ring the bell. We will leave you alone until you call. Come, my son."

They walked out, but Roberto looked back at Tracy and smiled shyly.

"You seem to have made a conquest," Marc said, ladling soup into her bowl.

"A little young for me, thanks." Tracy broke off a piece of crusty bread and spread it with butter.

"You like your men older, then?" An eyebrow arched above one eye, an action that had become very familiar to Tracy. It usually meant he was teasing or testing her. She ignored the remark and began to eat. She noticed that her hands were shaking. Hunger, that's all, she said to herself.

During the lamb stew course their conversation consisted of the typical small talk of two people learning about each other. The silences were comfortable; neither of them searched frantically for things to say. He asked where she came from, what her background was, and expressed surprise that she had been born in a very small Midwestern town. River Bend, Nebraska, he said, didn't seem her style.

She told him of her parents and her brother, Daniel. She saw a frown crease his forehead when she mentioned Vietnam, and she sensed that he wanted nothing more said about it. So she told him that River Bend's original name was Lying Squaw. He laughed and the dark look disappeared.

"I bet there were plenty of jokes about that."

"Yes, every schoolboy speculated on what kind of lying it referred to."

Two other couples entered, and Mama Valcarlos quietly welcomed them. They waved at Marc but didn't come over, sitting across the room and talking in low tones.

The dessert arrived, and Tracy was astonished by the amount of food she had eaten. The warm room, the rich food and the wine combined to make her feel mellow, almost disassociated from reality.

Tracy realized she had revealed more about herself than Marc had. She really knew very little about him. Where were his parents? Did he have any brothers or sisters? She started to ask him to tell her about himself when she paused, her head turned toward the door that led to the front of the house. At first the music was so faint that Tracy doubted she had heard it at all. Then it grew louder, suddenly flooding the room with a pulsating rhythm that reverberated through her body. Never before had Tracy been as inundated by sound as she was now; the resonant intensity made her heart echo the beat of the strings as Roberto strummed them, first in a hard, commanding way, then gently, as if he were wiping a tear from a child's cheek.

Then the melodies changed from classical to slow music that made Tracy sway with the tempo. Without knowing how it happened she was in Marc's arms and he was leading her to a small dance floor in one corner of the room. Tracy slipped one of her hands around Marc's neck, feeling his hair curl around her fingers. Her body molded his, their heights perfect for dancing.

He pulled her closer, making the contact more complete. From afar she could hear the strum of the lone guitar, but in her mind there was a full orchestra playing the slow, intimate music.

No word passed between Marc and Tracy; no words were needed as they moved to the mesmerizing notes that blocked out all other sounds. Tracy closed her eyes, fitting her head under Marc's chin. The sensual music filled her with strange erotic feelings. Taking a deep breath, she filled her lungs with the unique scent of the tall man who guided her in the steps of vertical lovemaking.

A sudden wave of emotions washed over her as Marc brushed his fingertips against her breasts. Her nipples strained against the silken fabric of her blouse; her desire for this stranger intensified to the point where she lost all concept of time. The walls disappeared. She was conscious only of this man and the heat of their joined bodies, aware only of how she wanted to remain in this surreal world, dancing to the music of love.

Marc lowered his face to hers and in between nibbling kisses around her ear whispered, "Roberto stopped playing five minutes ago."

Tracy leaned back in Marc's arms. "Hum?" she murmured, her voice husky and low. "What did you say?"

"I said . . ." His lips moved back down her cheek to the base of her neck and his tongue drew little circles there. ". . . the music has stopped. Let's get out of here. We'll continue this later . . ." He brushed her open lips with a soft kiss. ". . . don't lose the place."

Marc moved away from Tracy and, with his hand intertwined in hers, led her back toward the table. As they walked Tracy looked around, squinting in the dark room. The other people had left. "But where's Roberto?"

"That's what I've been trying to tell you. Rob has stopped playing, and we're leaving." He draped her shawl around her shoulders and led her to the front door.

"But I should tell Mrs. Valcarlos how much I enjoyed—"

"We'll see her again."

Before Tracy could say anything else they were out the door. The cold air hit her like a splash of ice water, and she started shivering. Marc paused on the stairs. "I should have left you in the house and warmed up the car. Why don't you go back inside?"

"No, I'll be all right. Just h-hurry." Marc lifted her, protecting her as best he could from the cold wind that whipped around them. By the time he had placed her in the car Tracy's shaking was uncontrollable, her teeth clicking together like castanets. Marc ran around to the other side, climbed in, started the motor and then pulled her toward him, enfolding her against his body. Like a kitten seeking a warm place to hide, Tracy's hand slipped around him and under his sweater. She could feel the pattern of his muscles through his shirt.

Marc rubbed her back and arms quickly at first, trying to warm her. Then his movements changed, became slower, and he obviously enjoyed the sensation of touching her through her sheer blouse. His lips found hers; tentatively at first, then with a surging passion, his mouth began to work its magic. He continued to rub her back, making occasional forays to her ribs, with quick teasing brush strokes on the sides of her breasts. Then his hands slid back and continued running up and down her spine.

One spot near her waist was so sensitive when Marc rubbed it that Tracy felt as if a bolt of electricity had shot through her. Moaning, she arched her body against his. Marc returned to that spot often. After a long time he pulled his mouth from Tracy's and with little tasting kisses moved to the lobe of her ear. "Warmer?" he whispered.

Tracy's shivering had stopped long ago. Her answer to his question was to snuggle closer. She knew she should end this, but the sensual pleasures his actions aroused felt too good.

Marc leaned over and turned on the heater; warm air filled the car. Tracy took the opportunity to move back and, with tremulous hands, flipped an errant curl from her forehead. Her breath came in short gasps, as if she'd run a long distance. A deep shuddering sigh helped calm her pounding heart. Marc started to move closer, but Tracy laid a hand on his chest to stop him. "Please . . . don't. Besides, I'm warmer now."

"I should say you are." Placing his hands on each side of her head he began to kiss her tenderly yet insistently, kisses that forced her to respond to his demands, to match his desire and passion. Without her knowledge Tracy's hand returned to Marc's back and she ran her nails down the hard muscles. From lips that were exploring the hollow of her throat came a low moan of pleasure.

She continued to trace her fingers down his spine, the pressure growing firmer, more urgent; unknowingly she was sending a message of sexual excitement. Marc lifted his head and looked at her. When she realized what her actions were doing to him she stilled her hand.

"Don't stop," he murmured and began to slip the cloth-covered buttons of her blouse through their slots, his hands moving slowly and carefully, as if he feared tearing the material. A frown of concentration formed a crease between his eyebrows; Tracy reached up and, with featherlike strokes, tried to erase the mark. He paused and looked at her, a smile tugging at one corner of his mouth.

"What's the matter?" he whispered.

"Nothing. You were so intent in your endeavors, you were frowning." She touched his forehead and tenderly rubbed away the lines.

Marc bent forward and ran his tongue along her smiling lips, then continued to open the third button. Tracy felt a smoldering glow spread through her as his fingers found and opened the front catch of her bra.

"Marvelous invention, that." He cupped a breast in one hand and rubbed the nipple with his thumb.

"Invented by a man, no doubt," she whispered.

He chuckled softly and bent down to rain kisses on the

full mound. His breath tickled her as his mouth captured her now taut nipple and tenderly pulled at the hard bud. An unbidden shiver of desire erupted deep in her being, and her breath came in short gasps.

Marc lifted his head and began to kiss her closed eyelids, her nose, her eager mouth while he boldly stroked her breast, his touch bringing a throbbing pleasure-filled pain that made Tracy want to lessen the distance between them. She moved against him with a force that took Marc by surprise. His back toward the door, he began to slip into the space in front of the steering wheel, pulling Tracy with him.

A loud, piercing sound sent Tracy rearing back. Her already racing heart shifted to a full gallop. She sat up and the noise stopped. The stillness that followed was nearly as deafening as the original blare. Looking around, confused, she knew what had happened: She had leaned on the car horn. Before she could stop herself she began to laugh.

"Damn! Did you do that on purpose?" Marc sat up, a scowl on his face.

Tracy could only shake her head no. "I—I'm sorry. . . ." No more words came, only laughter that brought tears to her eyes. With shaky fingers Tracy buttoned her blouse. Marc put the car in gear and in seconds they were racing down the highway. Seeing Tracy wipe the tears away with her fingers, Marc silently handed her a handkerchief, then concentrated on his driving.

Suddenly serious, Tracy looked at Marc's face, illuminated by the light from the moon. His dark eyebrows framed his intelligent eyes, made larger by thick black lashes. His face was kept from being too handsome by that slight bump in his nose. She almost asked him about it, but he wasn't smiling, so she refrained. Then, as Tracy watched, his scowl disappeared, his lips curved upward and he began to laugh. Enjoying the shared humor, Tracy saw no more of the passing scenery. When the car pulled into the driveway of Mille Fleur House she looked around in surprise.

"I think we had better postpone what we started tonight for a more opportune time and place," Marc said, cutting the engine. "Next time I'll make different arrangements."

Marc's words brought Tracy back to reality and reminded her of why she was in Brewster. What had happened to Tracy Cole, Super Executive, who had been so self-assured that she had convinced herself she could keep a businesslike attitude around Marc Durand? What had happened to that Tracy Cole? Well, for one thing, she told herself, she had been thoroughly, expertly and excitingly kissed by a man she found extremely attractive.

Marc interrupted her thoughts by opening her door and lifting her out. He climbed the marble stairs of the old house, swearing when his foot slipped on the ice and they nearly fell. He set Tracy down to open the large door, then led her inside.

"I can go on from here, thanks," Tracy whispered.

Marc took her arm and started up the stairs. "I always see my date to her door, just as my father instructed."

"I . . ." Tracy cleared her throat so her voice lost its huskiness. "I think you've found a fantastic cure for frostbite."

"We'll send word of our discovery to the medical association tomorrow." She could hear amusement in his voice. "But we might have to do more experimenting. Would you like to go outside and try again?"

"No, thanks."

At her bedroom door they stared at each other while

long moments ticked by. Tracy, suddenly embarrassed by Marc's close scrutiny, looked away and reached into the deep pocket of her skirt to find the key.

She turned and with shaky hands tried to fit the key in its slot. Marc took it from her fumbling fingers and unlocked the door, but didn't open it.

"Thank you." Tracy's voice was steady, masking her inner tension. "I had a lovely evening." She paused and then decided that she had better make some arrangements to show him Magnum's proposal. "About tomorrow, shall we try for 8:30 in the dining room for breakfast?"

He stepped closer, pressing Tracy's back against the door. "I meant to mention that. I can't meet with you this weekend. I'm going to Seattle." His fingers were gently touching her cheek, then running lightly over her lips, as if he were memorizing her face by touch. "We'll have to wait until Monday."

His words snapped Tracy out of her mellow mood. She almost shouted, "Monday!" and tried to move away from him. "I planned to leave on Monday."

Marc's arms closed around her, and he bent down to rain kisses along her eyelashes. She tried to push him away, but Marc drew her to him and said, "After you've been in the West for a while you'll learn that we operate at a much slower pace than you easterners."

The more Tracy struggled, the tighter Marc held her. "Besides, it'll give you time to see the fair town of Brewster."

"But Monday is two days—"

He stilled her angry words by giving her a deep, probing kiss that left her knees weak. He stepped back, but before releasing her he said, "Next time I try to make love to you, don't get the giggles. See you Monday."

He was down the hall and at the head of the stairs before Tracy could say another word. She watched him disappear from sight, then opened the door and entered her room.

Just as she had done that morning, Tracy walked to the window and rubbed a spot on the glass. As she watched Marc drive away, she whispered to herself, "Marc Durand, if you're playing a delaying game, you'd better have a good reason. I want no sellout to a higher bidder in Brewster."

4

When Tracy awoke the next morning she couldn't remember having spent a worse night. The heavy quilt and sheets were pulled out from the bottom of the bed and coiled in tight rolls, testimony to the myriad questions that had whirled in her mind: Why had Marc requested that a representative from Magnum rush here when he had to leave the next day? And why did he have to go to Seattle? Wasn't that where Mrs. Quartermain had said Elise Schell and her grandfather were? Was he going there to be with Elise? Why should she care what Marc did? Why did she enjoy Marc's company so much and think about him constantly when he was away? Why did she let him mesmerize her with his hands and mouth, leaving her breathless with desire? What was happening to her? Why was she acting like a lovesick teen-ager? She was *not* in love with Marc Durand. She had only known him for twenty-four hours. Something as important as love didn't happen that fast, at least not to Tracy Cole.

Last evening she had convinced herself that by having dinner with Marc Durand she could learn more about him as a person, more about his past, present and future, and perhaps determine how to deal with him. Instead, all she had discovered was that he could charm her as easily as an Indian fakir could lure a snake out of a basket. What would happen next time they met? How could she control the attraction she felt for him? And did she want to?

She had until Monday to contemplate her dilemma. Meanwhile, she needed to find something to do for two days in a strange, snowbound town. Dressing in warm ski clothes, Tracy decided that after breakfast she'd go to the square again. Perhaps the town had a theater. Or she could see the town hall and the library. All in all, the weekend didn't sound too exciting.

While Tracy ate her breakfast she read the new edition of the surprisingly complete weekly paper. International, national and local news items were succinctly and clearly written, the advertisements not overpowering, the pictures journalistically good. Tracy decided that she'd like to meet and compliment its publisher: Kent Regan. Tracy remembered the name. He was Marc's friend who had played with him at Mille Fleur House.

Mrs. Quartermain brought her bill. As Tracy signed her name she wondered what the accounting department would think of the low expense account she would present. If Magnum started a mine here, Tracy thought, prices would be sure to skyrocket.

"Thanks, Mrs. Quartermain. Tell Vivian it was delicious." She stood and added, "I'm on my way to the town square and the library. Do you suppose it's open today?"

The tiny woman said, "Yes, every day until five. We're a people who like to read. You see, we have no television reception here because of the mountains."

While they walked out of the dining room Mrs. Quartermain told her about the public library that Tobias Brewster had built on the square. "He set up a fund for acquisitions," she explained. "But his own books are stored here at Mille Fleur House, on the second floor. I'll be glad to show you around anytime."

"Thanks, I'd like that. I'll need a room for my meeting with Marc Durand. Perhaps we could use the library."

Mrs. Quartermain agreed, saying just to let her know.

Walking up the empty street toward the square, Tracy threw back the hood of her parka and enjoyed the sun's feeble warmth. The splashing of her boots in the melting snow was the only sound in the almost palpable silence. After the cacophony of New York, this utter quiet disconcerted Tracy, increasing her sense of unreality.

She wandered around town, looked in every shop, bought hot chocolate and five best-selling novels at the drug store, investigated the closed city buildings and visited the library. Eliminating the G-rated movie, she decided to go back to her room to read. On the way she saw a sign for Blanche's Beauty Salon. Having someone else wash and dry her hair would be a treat and a way to spend another hour of this boring day, she decided.

Later, after having dinner alone in the dining room, she returned to her bedroom and analyzed her one-sided conversation with Blanche Pomeroy, the broad-beamed, henna-haired town gossip who had known Marc, Kent and Elise since they were born. Tracy learned that the Durands, Schells and Regans had been among the first families to settle in Brewster. "Bedford County's elite," Blanche had called them. All of them, especially Marc's great-grandfather, had made their money from silver mining. Now Kent Regan owned the newspaper his family started in 1880, and Marc Durand was the big landowner.

Blanche had told her how Marc and Elise had "gone together" all through school and how Marc, Kent and Frank Harlow had been such good friends, separated only when Marc and Kent left for college. While they were gone Elise had surprised everyone by marrying Frank Harlow, the county sheriff. "Marc left town, went to San Francisco for a long time and brought back a bride of his own. But that didn't last. She hated Idaho and they've been divorced about five years."

"And he never remarried?" Tracy had asked. "I wonder why."

Blanche had laughed. "Oh, it's not been for lack of opportunity. The town's eligible women from eighteen to forty-five have all plotted to get him hooked, but so far he's slipped away. Perhaps he looked at Frank and Elise's marriage and shied away from trying again. If ever there was a union made in hell, that was one. Frank was constantly jealous of Marc, accusing him and Elise of having an affair behind his back. He was a man eaten up with jealousy, envy and hate." She had paused and shook her head as if confused by the vagaries of human emotions.

"The marriage lasted, surprising everyone. Frank was killed a year ago while out hunting. Now everybody is speculating about what happened on the mountain and who will marry the widow—Kent Regan or Marc Durand."

With these words Tracy had experienced a sensation of doubt and despair, reactions that surprised and shocked her. Now, as she slipped on her nightgown and climbed into bed, she remembered how stunned she had been by Blanche's remarks. Why was she so interested in what had happened on that hunting trip? Or in Marc's possible marriage to Elise? Why should she care? By next month she'd be concentrating on some other town, some other potential deal. Brewster and Elise Schell and Marc Durand would all be quickly fading memories by then.

Fluffing up the large pillows behind her head, Tracy made a valiant attempt to read, but absorbed nothing of the book's content. Images of Marc kept distracting her.

Finally she put the book aside to think about the times when she had been with him.

So far, in the thirty-six hours that she had known him, he had made her wait for his arrival, albeit with a good excuse; had insulted her, for which he had apologized; sexually courted her, to which she had responded with a surprising passion; and shunted her aside while he tended to "more important" business in Seattle, for which he had offered no explanation. Never before had she been treated in such a cavalier manner. Then, to learn that he might be contemplating marriage to Elise Schell . . . Tracy frowned, remembering his passionate attentions of Friday night. He certainly hadn't acted like a man who was about to be married. What game was he playing?

Still confused about her reactions to Marc, she turned out the light and fell into a troubled sleep, disturbed by dreams that she remembered only vaguely the next morning.

A light tapping on the door awakened her. She was still sleepy and hoped whoever was knocking would go away. But the noise continued, setting a rhythm that matched the faint pounding in her head.

"Just a minute," she called out. She climbed out of bed, slipped on a robe over her short gown and went to unlock the door.

Marc Durand was leaning against the door frame, arms crossed over his Aran Isle sweater, tight-fitting jeans encasing his legs.

"But I thought . . ."

Marc didn't let Tracy finish her sentence. Instead he took her in his arms, pressed her against his tall frame, lifted her so her feet didn't touch the floor and walked into the room, shutting the door with his foot. Tracy's first reaction was to coil her arms around his neck, but she didn't dare indulge herself. But the clean scent of this man—a fragrance that sent her senses reeling—made it difficult to remain impassive.

He nuzzled his head in her neck and murmured, "Holding you wearing a robe and nightgown is becoming a habit, isn't it?" He effectively prevented her from replying with a kiss that surpassed any he had given her before. While Marc's tongue tasted deeply of her mouth, Tracy experienced the return of the previous night's passion. Despite her best intentions, her body traitorously welcomed him back by responding to his kisses in a way that left no doubt as to her feelings.

Reality returned and Tracy refocused her mind on the fact that she was again falling under Marc's spell. She placed her hands on his chest and bent backward to remove her lips from the magnetic pull of his.

"Marc, stop kissing me and tell me what you're doing here." Her voice didn't sound as determined as she had hoped.

He released her, but kept his hands on her arms, as if he needed to touch her, to have her near him. "The weather was changing, so I finished up my business early."

"And just what was your business in Seattle?" The words were out before she could stop them, sounding angrier than she had intended.

Marc tilted his head curiously at her. He seemed amused by her question. "I flew there to pick up Elise and Tom. He'd gone to a clinic for medical treatment."

"Oh," she said in surprise. A little ashamed of her incorrect assumptions, she added, "I'm glad you came back." The sincerity in her voice surprised her. She *was* glad he had returned. To hide her embarrassment she said, "Perhaps now we can begin to discuss my proposal, and I can leave Monday or Tuesday."

Marc looked down at her and asked, "Why are you in such a hurry to go? Don't you find our little town exciting enough?"

She wanted to tell him that it was only exciting when he was there. With this thought, Tracy faced the reality of her problem: She wanted to be with Marc, to have him make love to her, to let the dizzying sensations she felt when he held her in his arms erase the memory of cobalt, sale contracts, Magnum—or Elise.

He seemed to read her thoughts, because he asked, "What's the matter? Worried about your role as lady executive? Surely some long-ago college professor explained what to do in a situation like this."

She looked away from his eyes so he could no longer see her confusion. Escaping his embrace, she walked to the bed, bending over to pull on her slippers over cold feet.

"Look, Marc, why don't you go downstairs until I'm dressed? We'll have breakfast and discuss business. Tomorrow morning I have to report your thoughts about Magnum's offer to my head office, and I can't very well say that so far I haven't even presented the proposal."

Marc looked at her, one eyebrow lifted. "I don't suppose you'd consider my staying here while you get dressed?"

Tracy's irritation increased. "Oh, sure. Lady Executive Deportment Class 1-A taught me that that was a sure way to win friends." Tracy pushed her hair back from her face. "Sorry, I flunked that class." No humor softened her voice.

"I see you're still upset about what I said Friday morning. What can I do to make you accept my apology?"

"You can get out of here and let me get dressed."

Marc's grin returned. "OK. I want to show you the

ranch, so wear something warm. Bring jeans and boots, if you have them. We might go riding."

"But I can't go to your ranch. I'm in Idaho for one purpose only, and it's not to go riding or sightseeing."

Marc said nothing, just walked over to her and ran his hands down her arms, looking intently into her eyes. Despite knowing that she should pull away from his disturbing nearness, his overpowering maleness, she longed to succumb to his entrancing power. Was she going to feel this torment every time he came near her?

Her quickening pulse revealed what he was doing to her senses. She spoke his name, wanting it to be a denial of his actions. Instead the word came out as a sigh of acquiescence. His strong arms continued to encircle her, and his warm hands moved around to her back. She instinctively melted closer to him and wondered if he could stop his exploration of her mouth without something further happening. Right now, she wasn't at all sure she cared.

But stop he did, and when he spoke his voice was husky and low. "Hurry. We have a lot to do today." In three long strides he was out of the room, leaving her alone to calm her racing heart.

Tracy shook her head, trying to clear her mind of Marc's disturbing presence. Then she rushed to her dresser, where she saw that it was 9:13, later than she had thought. Feeling a sense of excitement, she dressed in ski pants, sweater and snow boots. To keep her hair under control she deftly twisted the curls into a coil and piled it on top of her head. Instead of putting her sunglasses in her pocket, she set them in front of the crown of hair. Then she took several deep breaths to calm her quaking nerves. Never before had she felt so excited about meeting a man. But excited or not, she'd take the proposal down with her.

She was dressed and downstairs, walking into the dining room before her watch read 9:30. Marc rose courteously from his table near the window. Heads turned as she entered. Today the dining room was full of families, dressed in their Sunday best. Tracy felt a little out of place in her form-fitting sweater and ski pants.

"For someone who climbed out of bed only"—Marc looked at his watch before holding the chair for her—"seventeen minutes ago, you look very beautiful. But even if you are fast, I like you better in your robe."

Tracy placed her briefcase on the floor near her chair and looked over at him, a slight frown creasing her forehead. "I'll have to speak to Mrs. Quartermain about letting men on the third floor."

Marc grinned. "What are you going to eat? Personally, I'm starved." He concentrated on the menu while Tracy watched his face, trying to analyze him based on what Blanche had told her and on what little he had revealed of himself. She had a premonition that Marc wasn't entirely the fun-loving charmer he pretended to be. His handsome face, sparkling blue eyes framed by thick lashes, and strong, virile body all combined to present the image of a man who was sure of himself and his place in the world. Yet hidden deep in his eyes she saw a lonely man, a man searching for something and not sure where to find it.

Stop that, she admonished herself, realizing that she was surmising things she could not possibly know. Suddenly she became aware that Marc was staring at her with an intensity that matched her own. So complete was their concentration that they noticed nothing beyond what they read in each other's eyes.

Finally Marc spoke, his voice silky and low. "I'd give a hell of a lot to know what you were thinking."

Tracy gazed down and rearranged the napkin on her

lap. Her hands were steady, but she needed time to think of a response.

"I . . . uh . . . I was wondering how you could fly all the way from Seattle and get here so quickly." She raised her face, again looking directly at him.

"I have a fast plane and we left early." He paused, one eyebrow rising. "You know, Tracy Cole, you're very good. You lied yourself out of that with surprising ease." He reached for her hand and caressed the palm with his fingertips. "I think I'm going to enjoy working with you these next few weeks."

"Weeks!" she gasped, pulling her hand from his grasp. "What do you mean, weeks?"

Marc shrugged and, picking up his fork, drew zigzag lines on the table. "You can combine a vacation with this business trip. Enjoy yourself, have some fun. You said this was your first visit to Idaho."

"I haven't been sent here for fun or a vacation. I've come to see if you and Magnum can agree on terms for the sale of your land. And since we do have a great deal of material to cover"—Tracy bent down to pick up her briefcase—"we should start right now." She snapped open the latch and pulled out a thick silver-and-blue plastic folder. The familiar company colors reminded her of just how far she was from Magnum and her calm office, where everything was easy to keep in proportion. But since arriving here she had discovered emotions and sensations and passions that were foreign to her, and she knew what had brought them to the surface—the man sitting across the table, watching her with a bemused smile.

He reached out, took the folder and, without looking at it, set it on the table near him. Just then a teen-age waitress with braces and glasses stopped at their table and said, "Good morning, Miss Cole, Mr. Durand. What can I get you this morning?"

Marc and Tracy ordered, and while they waited Tracy reached for the folder, wanting to show him the environmental impact studies. But he moved it beyond her reach, saying, "Too early for that. I can't think without coffee and food."

Perhaps you can't think before breakfast, Tracy thought, but you can certainly attempt a little seduction. But to be honest, she had to admit that she hadn't protested too much. Forcing her thoughts away from that topic, she tried again to interest him in Magnum.

"We do have a great deal to go over. I think we should start now."

"Nope." There was finality in the word. "Now, tell me what you did while I was gone. Did you miss me?"

"Yesterday morning I treated myself and went to Blanche Pomeroy to have my hair washed and dried. She gave me the works."

He laughed, a deep, happy sound. "Oh, I'm sure she did." He chuckled again and leaned back in his chair. "What did she have to say?"

Before Tracy could answer their food arrived. Marc's steak sizzled on a metal platter set on an oval wooden board. The aroma of his food made her stomach growl hungrily, and without saying anything she began to butter her pancakes. They were silent until the edge was taken off their hunger. Then Marc looked up and said, "Well, who did Blanche talk about this time?"

"Oh, Marc, it was just a bored woman's idle gossip."

Marc placed his knife and fork down on his plate and waited for her to continue.

"Well . . . she told me how you and Frank and Kent were such good friends in school and what hellions and practical jokers you were and . . ." Her voice trailed off; she didn't want to continue.

"And all about Frank Harlow's jealousy and hate, his unhappy marriage and his death, right?"

Tracy nodded reluctantly. "Well, yes. I walked in and became a captive audience—someone with a wet head who hadn't heard her stories before. I tried to stop her, but . . ."

"But you learned that nothing could still her tongue." Wry amusement was in his voice. "She loves to talk about Brewster's tragedies."

Marc sprinkled more pepper on his over-easy eggs and began to eat again, apparently no longer interested in the subject, much less in explaining the incident that had occurred a year ago.

Tracy pushed her plate away and said quietly, "What happened up on the mountain?"

Marc looked up and set his fork down, contemplating his words. "If you talked to Blanche, you know most of the background. A year ago Frank's attitude changed, as if he finally saw that his jealousy of me was unfounded. When Kent and I agreed to go hunting with him, it was like old times." He shook his head, as if the memories were too painful. "Frank spotted an eight-point buck, tracked it and never returned to camp. When we found him, he was dead . . . we still don't know if it was accidental or on purpose."

"How terrible for Elise." Tracy longed to ask Marc if he loved Elise and what his feelings toward her were now that she was a widow. But she couldn't. If Marc wanted her to know, he'd tell her. Until he did, she could only speculate.

Looking out the window, she concentrated on the river at the bottom of the garden, wanting to go outdoors, to smell the air filled with the scent of pine, to hear the wind whistle its song through the trees. But most of all, she wanted to spend the day with Marc Durand, to have him show her his world. But she couldn't; she had to get him to hear her proposal today.

"Mrs. Quartermain said we could work in the library

here at Mille Fleur House. Before we go to the ranch, let's—"

Marc stood and came around to her chair. "Today is Sunday. And it's against Idaho rules to work on Sunday. Besides, Tracy Amanda Cole, I have a day planned for you . . . a day you'll remember for a long time."

5

~~~~~~~~~~~~

While Marc stayed in the foyer talking to Mrs. Quartermain, Tracy went upstairs to get the clothes she would need for a day at the ranch. As she climbed the two flights of stairs she made a decision that she hoped she wouldn't regret. If Marc persisted in his refusal to discuss Magnum and if he had prepared an "unforgettable" day for her, so be it. She would go along with his plan, but tomorrow . . . tomorrow she must conduct company business. She would accept no more of his manipulations, no more delays or attempts to sidetrack her. And she would tell him of her decision at the first opportunity.

Pleased that she had finally straightened the situation out in her mind, Tracy entered the bedroom with a feeling of relief. Today she would enjoy herself. Tomorrow she'd go to work.

In a small bag she packed jeans, a shirt and the western boots she had bought in New York the year before. Never knowing what to expect on business trips, Tracy had a tendency to bring a wide variety of clothing—everything from supercasual to ultradressy. The riding clothes had been a last-minute addition, and she was pleased she had remembered.

Tracy picked up her handbag but left the briefcase, knowing it would do no good to bring it. Ready at last, she turned out the light and locked the door.

As she descended the stairs, Tracy stopped halfway down to the main floor. Marc stood close, very close, to a woman whose back was turned; all Tracy could see was a slender figure encased in burgundy slacks and sweater that were molded seductively to her body. Pale flaxen hair was pulled back and fell halfway down her back.

Marc looked up and saw Tracy watching them. He smiled and beckoned to her to come down, saying something to the woman, who then turned toward Tracy. No smile lightened her somber yet beautiful face.

"Tracy Cole," Marc said as she neared them, "this is Elise Schell."

Both said the correct words of greeting; both eyed the other warily. Tracy reached out and they shook hands.

"I hope everything is satisfactory with your room, Miss Cole."

"Oh, yes, thanks." Tracy smiled, her gaze slipping over to Marc. His face was unreadable, as if he were an observer, detached and impersonal.

"Good. Perhaps tomorrow you could come to my apartment on the second floor and meet my grandfather. We could talk then. I understand that your schedule is full today." She looked tired, and an aura of sadness surrounded her. She turned to Marc and said, "Have fun, and congratulations again. You always win, don't you?" Her gaze returned to Tracy. "Goodbye, Miss Cole. I'll plan on seeing you tomorrow. Nice meeting you." Elise quickly walked away.

"Come on," Marc said. "Let's get out of here before Mrs. Quartermain corners me again." He took her arm and propelled her toward the door.

Marc was using the red pickup truck today, and as Tracy walked around the back a huge black shape covered with long hair lumbered to its feet and barked loudly.

"Okay, Daphne, she's a friend," Marc shouted. The noise stopped immediately and the dog leaned over the side of the truck and sniffed. As it seemed to accept Tracy it actually grinned with friendliness, its breath puffing clouds into the cold air.

"Her name can't be Daphne," Tracy said, climbing up into the cab.

"Well, it is. I named her Daphne because she reminded me of a nurse I knew in the Marines."

"That's not very flattering to the poor nurse—to name your dog after her."

"If you'd seen the nurse you'd know it's Daphne who should be insulted."

The motor roared, and Daphne began to bark, making conversation difficult. To be heard, Tracy moved closer to Marc and yelled, "What kind of dog is she?"

"Newfoundland." He shifted into first gear and headed down the driveway. Before Tracy could slip back to her side of the truck, Marc drew her to him and grinned. "I like you near me."

Tracy didn't move back. Whenever the car turned a corner, she was excitingly aware of how her thigh was pressed against his.

They drove without speaking, listening to Daphne loudly proclaim her superiority to the world. Finally Marc slowed down and slid open the glass panel between the cab and the back.

"Daphne! Stop that barking. Lie down!" Tracy was amazed to see a hurt expression on Daphne's face. The dog barked one last time, as if asking Marc to reconsider, then was quiet.

As they drove out through the canyon that sheltered

the town, the steep mountains gave way to an alluvial plain that spread out like a fan before meeting gently rolling hills. Out here, there were fewer trees. Sagebrush and grass showed through dirty and trampled snow. Hereford and black Angus cattle lifted their heads to watch the red truck pass, never changing the rhythm of their chewing.

Because of Daphne, Tracy had gleaned another bit of information about Marc. He had been wounded in the Marines. How? Where? She'd probably never know. Remembering the strange look he had given her when she had commented on her brother's death in Vietnam, she sensed that Marc wouldn't welcome any personal questions about his past.

Wanting to learn something about him, even so, she asked, "What did Elise mean when she said you always win?"

"You'll see."

Well, Tracy thought, he certainly knows how to avoid answering questions.

Marc kept driving until they pulled into a large parking area in front of a redwood and fieldstone house.

Daphne barked happily and bounded out of the truck, taking off toward a large red barn, acting like a huge puppy released from its pen.

Tracy jumped out of the cab. "What a magnificent house," she said, awed by the design that blended in with the countryside so effectively that it seemed an extension of the rolling hills that surrounded it. Nearby a small river wound through groves of birch and quaking aspen.

A man walked toward them, carrying a bucket. He had a cigarette in his mouth and squinted his eyes against the smoke. Marc introduced him as Fred.

"Ma'am." He nodded, then turned toward Marc. "Andy said a section of fence is down over by Holy Rock."

"OK." Marc thought for a moment, then said, "Tracy and I'll go riding this morning instead of later. I'll check it out. Get Whisper saddled, and Suzette." He turned to Tracy. "Come on in. You'll need to change your clothes."

Fred followed Daphne's route to the barn. Marc carried Tracy's shoulder bag and duffel and, taking her arm, led her up the walkway to ten-foot-tall double doors. The front hall was dim after the brightness outside. Before Tracy's eyes had a chance to adjust Marc put his hand against the small of her back and guided her past a dining room on the left and a living room on the right. They walked down a long hall, their footsteps muffled by the thick beige carpet. Tracy wished Marc would slow down so she could see more of the house. Suddenly they turned left down another hall and Marc opened a bedroom door. As they entered he switched on a dresser lamp, set her things down on a nearby chair and turned to Tracy.

"You can change here. I'll be back." He quietly shut the door.

Tracy took off her parka and bent down to free her feet from the confining warmth of her heavy snow boots, then examined the room. The simply designed heavy wood furniture and the warm earth tones were in keeping with what she had seen of the rest of the house. She pushed open the heavy drapes that covered a large window and stared at the view of the mountains. From this distance they seemed less formidable, but still awesome.

Entranced by the scene, she stood for a long time, staring at the saw-toothed peaks. Finally turning away, she pulled off her ski pants and bent down to open her duffel. Then she heard a knock and looked up to see the door opening. Marc stood in the doorway. An involuntary gasp escaped Tracy's lips, and she could think of no coherent words to say to this man who filled the room with his aura of masculinity.

"I'm sorry, Tracy. I thought you were a fast dresser." His gaze roamed over her half-clad body, and Tracy could see the desire in his eyes.

Her heart shifted to a new rhythm, and deep inside she ached with a strange longing. Surprised and shocked by her instantaneous physical response to Marc's presence, she turned her head so he couldn't see her own desire.

Tracy realized that she must act, must do something to break this spell. "Give me just a minute to finish getting dressed," she said with a calmness that belied her tension.

"Tracy, I . . ." Marc whispered, his voice low with emotion. Then he walked into the room, holding a hand out toward her. Tracy longed to cross the distance that separated them, to be pulled against his body and held there forever. But she held back. Some instinct warned her to restrain the urge to go to him.

Turning her back on him, she began to pull on her denim jeans. Deliberately misinterpreting his invitation, she said, "It's all right, Marc; you don't have to apologize. I should have been ready. I'll be dressed in a minute." Her voice was cool and didn't reveal her inner conflict.

Without looking at Marc she zipped her jeans. Finally she dared to look around. He had silently moved from the center of the room and now lay on the bed, leaning against the backboard, two arms behind his head, long legs casually crossed, watching her with an intensity that disturbed her. Then he smiled. "I said before that you were good at getting out of uncomfortable situations. You just proved it again."

"I don't know what you mean," she said, bending down to tug on a boot.

"I've got to hand it to you. You didn't get flustered or

hysterical when I walked in and found you delightfully half dressed."

"I told you before, I'm not the hysterical type. Besides, I should be used to finding you in my bedroom by now." Tracy emphasized the words by stamping her foot into her tight boot. She heard Marc chuckle.

Walking toward the bed to get her parka, she said, "I'm ready."

Her gaze locked with Marc's and she could read his longing for her. With a languorous movement he reached out and wrapped his fingers around her wrist. His strength denying her attempt to stop him, he guided her hand to his lips and gently kissed the palm. Tracy tried to pull away, but using steady, insistent pressure he drew her down on the bed beside him. He rolled toward her and pinned one of her arms under his body; the other was held by the side of her head.

"When I walked in and saw you standing there in that sweater and those lace panties all I could think about was continuing what we started in the car the other night. I wanted you to come to me and let me make love to you. You wanted it too, didn't you?"

Tracy shook her head in denial. "You saw what you wanted to see." She tried to rise, but couldn't move.

"I saw that you wanted me to slip off that sweater and your easily opened bra, and then take off the wisp of lace that hid so little of your extremely nice body."

"That's not true," she whispered, knowing she was lying. She had wanted to go to him, to be enveloped in his arms.

Marc's lips found hers, and long moments passed as he thoroughly explored her mouth. They were both breathless when he pulled away.

"Tell me how much you wanted me to touch you here . . ." He cupped her breast, rubbing it and molding

73

it gently. ". . . and here . . ." His hand moved down and slipped under her sweater to touch the bare skin of her stomach. ". . . and here . . ." His hand slid past her waist, over her hips and down to her denim-clad legs. Each time he touched her a wave of sensations surged through her. She felt like a mindless creature that responded to the physical stimuli Marc so cunningly transmitted.

Marc changed positions, releasing his tight hold so he could run his fingers up and down the inside of her thighs. Without stopping this action he looked deeply into her eyes, and Tracy knew what he could see there. With each stroke of his hand her resolve to deny him weakened. Every nerve sang a message to shed her constricting clothes so she could feel his hands and mouth on her skin.

"Tracy. Tracy. Tracy." He didn't kiss her as he said her name, just maddeningly brushed her lips with each word. If her hands had been free she would have wound them around his neck, pulling him tightly to her.

"Tell me, Tracy. Say you want me to make love to you. Say it."

"Yes." The word passed her lips before the realization of its truth registered in her brain. A fleeting thought came that she would probably regret that admission. But that was for the future. Right now she only knew that she wanted him to make love to her.

Marc interrupted her thoughts by rising from the bed. He reached out his hand, and without hesitation Tracy grabbed it and allowed him to pull her up so she stood before him. He took off the sunglasses that had served as a tiara for her crown of hair and set them on the table near the bed. With the removal of the hairpins masses of auburn and gold curls tumbled down, looking like a waterfall of silken strands. Marc smoothed the hair away from her face and lightly kissed her.

Placing his hands on Tracy's hips he pulled her tightly against him. She knew she had aroused him and gloried in knowing she possessed this wondrous and mysterious power. His arms encircled her body, and Tracy placed her own around his neck, leaning back in order to look into Marc's smoke-blue eyes that were filled with desire for her. No longer did his lips seek hers. Instead he seemed content to examine her face while his hands roamed over her back. Finally he said, "I like the freckles across your nose." He bent down and scattered tiny kisses wherever he found them.

Tracy closed her eyes. Each kiss increased her feelings of expectation and excitement. Then Marc again pulled back. Tracy opened her eyes and watched his mouth form a half smile.

"Yes, Tracy Cole," he whispered, "I can see by those odd-colored eyes that you do indeed want me to make love to you." He kissed the end of her nose. "But I regret to say we can't now." Tracy started to speak, but Marc placed his fingertips against her mouth.

"Remember, pleasure is always increased by anticipation . . ." Before Tracy could express her growing anger Marc bent down, picked up her parka and placed it around her shoulders.

Tracy was stunned. To build her up to such an emotional level . . . and then to stop. There was a name for that.

"You play strange games, Marc Durand. You make up the rules as you go, and the other player has to follow your lead."

Anger, chagrin and embarrassment sharpened her voice. What a fool she'd been. She had willingly entered his game, had participated wholeheartedly, had asked for no assurances of fair play. But she had learned something. The next time she played one of Marc's games she'd know the rules beforehand. And Marc just might find out that his opponent was stronger than he thought, with a few surprises of her own.

They left the bedroom and retraced their earlier route, heading toward the front hall. Before Marc opened the door he turned to Tracy. "Don't be angry. You'll see that my game will be worth waiting for. Besides, Kent Regan insisted on coming over this morning to meet you." He placed his lips on Tracy's, whispering and kissing her at the same time. "When I make love to you, I don't want any doorbell to ring." He stepped back and placed his hand on the knob. "I've been guilty of poor planning twice now. I won't let it happen again."

Marc pulled open the door and escorted Tracy out into the crisp air. As they walked down the gravel path toward the stable Tracy looked around. Gray clouds obscured the sun, subduing all colors to muted shades. Neither Daphne nor Fred was in sight.

The cold breeze made Tracy shiver, and she reached in her pocket for her gloves and found a few hairpins. Quickly twisting her hair into one strand, she adroitly coiled and pinned it on top of her head. Marc watched her, amusement showing in his eyes. "I like you to wear your hair up. It's so nice to take out the pins and watch it tumble down around your shoulders." His voice had taken on that low, seductive quality again.

Tracy looked around, wanting to avert any further display of his passion. "What's the surprise you mentioned . . ." She paused and added, ". . . or did I receive it back in the bedroom?"

Marc laughed as he reached to push open the sliding doors of the stable. Taking her arm, he guided her inside. Tracy breathed in the pleasant smell of hay and animals, leather and liniment. The white-painted stable was extremely clean and tidy. One horse snorted a greeting, stamping its foot for attention. While Marc slid the doors shut he said, "Sounds like you still haven't forgiven me for calling time out." He took her hand in his own large one, intertwining their fingers. "I have lots of surprises for you today. And the first one is right here in this stall."

Tracy leaned over the half door, straining to see in the dim light. Standing near a mare was a foal, its still wobbly legs looking much too long for the rest of its body.

"Oh, how beautiful," Tracy whispered. "How old is it?"

"Born just before I came into town. I thought you'd like to name him."

The mare had a shiny roan-colored coat with the distinctive dark, leopard markings of an Appaloosa. The colt's coloring was much the same, but the spots on his rump resembled large raindrops. Marc leaned against a partition between the stalls and crossed his arms, waiting patiently while Tracy examined the foal. She wanted to touch the colt, but was afraid his mother might not like it. Instead she petted the docile mare's head, rubbing the velvet of her nose. Finally she turned and said, "Cobalt! That's his name."

Marc stood straight and shouted, "Cobalt!" At the sound, the startled mare whinnied and the colt moved closer to his mother's legs.

"Cobalt." Marc repeated the word as if he couldn't believe his ears. "Why, for God's sake?"

"Because cobalt is why I'm in Idaho and cobalt blue is the color of your eyes. Don't you like it?" She smiled sweetly, knowing from the tone of his voice that he didn't.

"No, I don't. Think of another," Marc grumbled.

"Cobalt is from 'kobold,' a German word meaning 'spirit' or 'goblin.' How about Goblin?"

"Well . . ." Marc thought for a moment and said, "OK, Goblin is fine." He smiled at Tracy and the feeling of warm intimacy she had experienced before returned. They stood staring for a long moment; then slowly some unknown force pulled her closer to him. She felt her body melting toward him and knew that as soon as their lips met their earlier passion would be reignited. He didn't even have to touch her for desire to emerge like a tiny flower bud, waiting for him to open the petals.

Marc stepped closer; his arms encircled Tracy's pliant body, and his mouth descended to capture her willing lips.

"Marc? You there?" A man's voice accompanied the sound of the stable doors being shoved open. Marc stepped back, but found Tracy's hand.

"Kent? Come on in and meet two of Idaho's newest arrivals." Tracy admired his cool manner.

She could distinguish nothing of the tall man's appearance until he walked into the circle of light. A blond man, even larger than Marc, dressed in the usual attire of western men—jeans, plaid wool shirt, boots and cowboy hat—stood looking down at her. He seemed older than Marc, with sad, deep-set eyes that were in contrast to the smile he directed toward Tracy. A deep resonant voice said, "Well, Tracy Cole, I've heard so much about you, I feel I already know you." He held her hand in both of his and showed an open friendliness that made Tracy immediately like and trust him.

"And from whom did you hear all about me?"

"Oh, from lots of people . . ." His smile deepened and lightened his eyes. He looked over at Marc. Tracy followed his gaze; Marc was intently watching the two of them, his familiar frown creasing his brow.

What could Marc have told Kent? Suddenly Tracy saw how mistaken she had been to let her emotions break down the wall she had built to keep men at a distance. She had even been foolish enough to convince herself that on Monday she could easily slip back into her businesslike pose and coolly, unemotionally present Magnum's offer for Marc's land. Not wanting either of the men to see her sudden confusion, Tracy pulled her hand out of Kent's, turned toward the stall and said, "Come meet Goblin."

All three leaned on the wooden stall door, watching the foal testing out his long legs. His attempts were made more difficult by the mare, who licked him every time he got close, nearly knocking him over. Marc and Kent became engrossed in discussing the mare and didn't seem to notice Tracy's inattentiveness.

"Damn you, Marc, you always were too lucky for your own good. You win a beauty like this mare, ready to drop her foal, on a poker hand. And then, if that isn't bad enough, you win it by bluffing. No wonder no one around here wants to play poker with you."

Marc laughed and shrugged, saying, "Some have it and some don't."

Tracy remembered Elise's remark at Mille Fleur House about Marc always winning. His luck seemed to extend to any game he played, be it poker or seduction.

Marc moved closer to Tracy, placing his hand on her arm in a proprietary manner that she found strangely disturbing. It was almost a display of ownership, a way of saying that Tracy was his. Even though his touch still thrilled her and made her physically aware of him, she tried to slip her arm away, but he drew her closer, turned toward Kent and said, "Do you want to go riding with us?"

"Sure. That is, if Tracy doesn't mind." Kent smiled at the two of them.

Tracy certainly didn't mind. In fact, she welcomed a neutral third party, knowing she didn't dare be alone with Marc for any length of time. She was seeing him in a new light—as a man who knew what he wanted and took it. Today *she* seemed to be what he wanted. But for how long would she hold his interest?

With an efficiency born of years of practice Kent

saddled and mounted a horse and was ready to go in a surprisingly short amount of time. Marc helped Tracy into her saddle, adjusted her stirrups and checked the reins. Again Marc's nearness made Tracy's pulse quicken. Looking down at him while he worked, she wondered if he were conscious of the tension between them. Could he be remembering the kisses they had shared, the passion he had aroused in her? Nothing showed on his face as he grinned up at her, his hand on her knee. "OK?"

"Yes, I'm fine," she lied. "Fine" was the last word she would use to describe her state of being. "Bewitched" and "confused" might be better ones.

"Good." Marc loaded his saddlebag with a hammer and U-shaped brads, caught the reins of his own horse and gracefully swung his leg across the saddle, easily controlling the large stallion. "You two ride out to the swimming hole, Kent. I have some fence I want to check over by Holy Rock. I'll meet you later."

Letting the horses set their own leisurely pace, Tracy and Kent turned in the direction opposite that of the now disappearing Marc. Daphne suddenly appeared and chased after him, barking at every shadow.

Tracy was the first to speak. "I think you publish a fine paper, Kent. It must be difficult in a community as isolated as Brewster is."

"Thanks." He paused and added, "Wire services help, of course. The difficult part about the job is choosing the most important national and international news and still leaving room for local events." He shook his head. "Every 4-H group, the Future Farmers of America and the Brewster Quilting Society want coverage."

Tracy laughed, enjoying the slow rhythm of her horse's walk. Finally her curiosity wouldn't be ignored, and she had to ask, "What did Marc say about me?"

Kent smiled knowingly, then reached down and patted

80

his horse's neck, taking his time before answering Tracy's question. They were following the twisting course of the river, going around thick clumps of aspen and willows. As the water tumbled over the rocks its music accompanied the song of the gentle wind that danced through the bare branches. The morning smelled of sage and pine. Even though they were miles away the snow-dappled mauve, purple and lavender hills shimmered with sparkling clarity. Tracy waited for Kent to speak, enjoying the scenery that was so different from Nebraska or New York. She felt as if she had truly entered another world, a world barely changed by man.

At last Kent cleared his throat and spoke, "You know, Tracy, Marc is a hard person to understand sometimes. He's a loner in many ways . . . never remarried after his divorce." He paused, then continued. "He likes the company of many women—for a while, but chooses none permanently." Kent shook his head, his expression somber.

"Marc's a complex and stubborn man who lives by his own inflexible code of rules, a man who likes to win, whether it be a poker game, a beautiful woman or a power struggle."

Tracy sensed that Kent had forgotten she was there; he was thinking only about his friend. The horses stopped at a bend in the river and nibbled the grass that still showed green through the patches of snow. Kent continued his story.

"Marc was in the Marines in Vietnam. He went there a boy and came back a man. I guess he just saw too much. Too much pain, too much agony." Kent stood in his stirrups to scan the horizon, the leather creaking loudly in the still air. He sat again, wound the reins loosely around the pommel and leaned back, his hands on the cantle behind him.

"Marc was wounded over there and shipped home.

When he got out of Oak Knoll Hospital in California he returned determined to keep Bedford County as untouched and pristine as it was in Tobias Brewster's time. He's spent the last few years working to keep it that way. It's almost an obsession with him." He smiled at Tracy. "I don't envy you your task in trying to convince Marc to sell that wilderness area."

A chill coursed through Tracy, accompanied by a flashing vision of the coming confrontation with Marc. The two of them had been playing a waiting game, knowing that the battle lines would soon be drawn with him on one side and her, as the Magnum representative, on the other.

The faint sound of someone calling their names made them turn. Marc was riding in their direction, shouting for them to join him upriver.

"Kent, you haven't answered my question. What did he say about me?"

Kent gathered his reins, guiding his horse onto the trail. "Marc never says much about anything or anyone. But Friday morning, after he left you in the dining room of Mille Fleur House, he came to the newspaper office and talked about you for over an hour—praising your spirit and looks and then cussing 'cause you're a career woman with a mind of her own." Kent laughed. "You sure made an impression."

"And what about Elise?" The words were out before she could stop them.

The same sad smile returned and he sighed. "Elise Schell?" He spoke in a whisper. "Nobody understands Elise Schell."

Before Tracy could ask Kent to explain Marc joined them, expertly reining in his lathered horse.

"Come on, Kent, let's show Tracy the swimming hole." Excitement shone in his eyes. "We used to skinny-dip there on hot summer days."

Kent smiled, as if remembering happy times. "And ice-skated there on cold winter ones."

The pond was surrounded by huge cottonwood trees with the previous spring's untidy birds' nests precariously sitting in the gnarled branches. After watching rainbow trout swim lazily in the clear water, the three of them continued their ride, the men taking turns telling her about the ranch and the history of the area.

It was nearly one o'clock before they got back to the house. Tracy's legs were wet and splattered with mud, and her thigh muscles were beginning to ache. Jogging around the roof of her apartment building hadn't prepared her for the bone-rattling rhythm of a broad-backed horse.

Back in the bedroom Tracy changed into her ski pants, freshened her makeup and rebraided her hair. Then she returned to the living room, where she sat in a large leather chair and watched Marc light the fire. The room, with its thick-beamed ceilings, had two focal points, and by swiveling her chair Tracy could see both the huge stone fireplace and the floor-to-ceiling windows that framed the majestic mountains in the distance. On the opposite wall was a bar where Kent now stood, pouring whiskey into a cut-glass tumbler. He looked over at Tracy and held up the decanter, a questioning look in his eyes.

"No, thanks, Kent. I'm fine." She turned back and faced the fire, stretching her legs in front of her. Marc walked over, placed his hands on the arms of the chair and bent down, looking deeply into her eyes.

"What can I get you? How about a brandy?" The softly spoken words and his nearness made Tracy's heart pound in her chest, and she felt an urge to reach out and touch him. She couldn't speak, just shook her head negatively.

"Hungry?" He leaned closer, his expression showing tenderness mingled with desire.

Determined not to let him know how his presence affected her, Tracy forced herself to relax, rested her head on the back of the chair and looked up at him. "Yes, I am. But remember, I don't cook. Do you?"

Marc smiled, took her hand in his and helped her to stand. "No, I don't, but Kent does. We'll watch him fix omelettes."

After they finished eating Tracy refilled their coffee cups and said, "Why do the Schells want to sell the mountain?"

Kent and Marc looked at each other, a silent message passing between them. Neither spoke, and they quickly looked down at their plates. Finally Kent said, "Elise is determined to preserve Mille Fleur House, and the money is running out."

Marc drank his coffee, pushed back his chair and set his plate and cup in the sink. "Come on. Let's get the snowmobiles and show Tracy the mine and the ghost town of Patience."

"Not me. I'm a working man." Kent seemed relieved at the interruption.

Tracy remembered Blanche's words: "Everybody in town is speculating who will marry the widow—Kent Regan or Marc Durand." Whom did she love? Was this the reason for their unwillingness to talk about Elise? Before Tracy could analyze the situation she found herself walking toward the front of the house. Marc held her arm possessively while they listened to Kent's explanation of why he couldn't stay.

"I have the dubious honor of reporting on and photographing Avery Coleman's sow and her record-breaking litter. Believe me, I would rather go with you two." He took Tracy's hand, bent down and lightly kissed her cheek. "Come by my apartment or, better yet, come to the newspaper office. It's next to the bank, across from the square. I'll give you a tour of the *Brewster Times* publishing complex, all two rooms of it." He turned toward Marc and said, "She's special. Watch yourself." He walked out the door, moving toward a yellow Ford parked beside Marc's truck.

Marc waved, shut the door, then turned to Tracy. "OK, mining-town tour or continuing where we left off?" His eyes had a mischievous gleam that warned Tracy she had better make it clear right now that she planned on changing the game to one in which she had more control. No more playmate of the day, she thought, trying unsuccessfully to pull her hand away.

"Definitely the mining town. Is Patience near the mountain so I can see where the cobalt is?" Before Tracy realized what he was doing, Marc had moved closer and was lowering his mouth to hers.

"Marc, stop that!" Tracy tried to step away, but he easily bent her hand behind her back and drew her body close to his.

"That town has been there a hundred years. It can wait a while longer." He began to guide her down the hall toward the bedroom. A feeling of near panic set in. Once she was in that room where she had so easily acquiesced to Marc's lovemaking she knew she'd be lost. Marc relaxed his hold on her hand, and Tracy slipped her fingers out. In a quick movement she turned and walked into the living room, heading for the chair where she had left her parka.

"Tracy?" She paused and turned. Marc stood by the door, an expression of puzzlement on his face.

"Marc, what happened before Kent came . . . well, it just happened . . ." Tracy watched him come slowly toward her, and she took an unconscious step back. "I . . ." She cleared her throat, which suddenly felt as dry as sandpaper. "I think we had better stop playing your game and begin one of mine. It's called Magnum

Representative Presents Proposal to Potential Seller. The rules are simple."

Marc was now standing very near her, his expression a combination of amusement and interest. He didn't touch her, just stood watching with one arched eyebrow.

"Yes? Go on."

Tracy couldn't find the words. He was too close, too compelling. She was angry with herself for having so little control over her emotions. Whenever she was within touching distance of Marc she lost all sense of the rational. No man had ever affected her so strongly.

"Marc, please understand, I . . ."

"For someone who can be so articulate, you certainly have a difficult time talking to me, but I think you're trying to tell me that it's too soon for you. OK, I'm a patient man. I can wait. Let's go find that ghost town."

6

Marc loaded the snowmobiles into the back of the truck and drove for miles over rutted roads, if they could be called roads, before coming to the base of a mountain. There he taught Tracy how to start her snowmobile, how to lean her weight into the turns and, most important, how to stop.

Soon Tracy felt confident enough to follow Marc's lead. The kaleidoscope of trees and rocks whizzing past exhilarated her, made her feel free and lighthearted. It took over an hour of climbing a rugged canyon, zigzagging, weaving and dodging around huge boulders and gigantic pine trees, before they reached a plateau. Spread below them was a view that made Tracy dizzy. She silently turned around, awed at the magnificence of the scene.

"It's unbelievable, Marc. I've never seen anything like this."

"You mean you lived in Nebraska and never went to Colorado to see the Rockies?"

"No. We always went East, to visit my grandmother in St. Louis. Or to Chicago, so Mother could take me to the museums and plays and concerts. I've seen pictures, of course, but they don't even come close to this." She spread her arms, turning around again to view the panorama of mountains and valleys, the streams of water tumbling out of canyons so steep that the sun never reached the deepest recesses.

Marc walked up behind Tracy, put his arms around her and drew her against him. The nylon of his jacket rustled in her ear. "I'm glad I was the first to show it to you. Once you've seen this you'll be under its spell; you'll never be the same again." Slowly, tentatively, as if afraid of her reaction, he turned Tracy so she faced him and looked into her eyes. "Let me welcome you to the mountains." Tenderly he placed his lips on hers in a simple, friendly kiss that conveyed none of the passion he had shown before. Tracy returned the kiss, keeping it on the same level. Marc was the first to pull back, a smile lifting one corner of his mouth.

When he spoke his voice was low, and Tracy felt her excitement return. "My God, Tracy Cole, if you knew what you do to me . . ." Taking a deep breath, he led her back to the snowmobiles.

"Come on, let's go." He smiled. "Patience is waiting."

The still air was again filled with their noise as Marc led the way. Finally he slowed and carefully began to weave his way down another canyon. Not far below the plateau, nestled in a pocket formed by two sides of the mountain, were buildings with wooden sides bleached to a shiny silver. Marc pointed out the assay office and the two-story hotel, but said they were too dangerous to enter. The snow gave the deserted town a peaceful look, as if it were sleeping, waiting only for the rowdy inhabitants to return from the mine.

Nearby was a graveyard encircled by a metal fence that tilted at an odd angle. Tracy read one of the faint inscriptions on a small carved stone: FRANKLIN FAIRMAN.

RICHMOND, VA. DIED FEB. 1886. AGE 22 YRS, 4 DYS. R.I.P.

"It was a young man's game, working in the mine," Marc said softly. "Few grew old."

He then showed Tracy the Patience Mine entrance, now blocked by rubble and thick brush.

"They took fourteen and a half million dollars worth of silver from the Patience Mine before it ran out. This is where Brewster got the money to build that monument to his own ego, Mille Fleur House, and the rest of the town. He used cheap Chinese labor brought in from San Francisco and paid them a third of what a white laborer got."

Tracy could detect bitterness in his voice as he went on. "Tobias Brewster and the others were takers, raping the land and leaving when the mines wouldn't give any more. Then Brewster built this town and became its ruler."

Why didn't Marc mention his own ancestor's part in the rape of the land? Blanche had said the three leading families—Regans, Durands and Schells—all got their money from the mine. Perhaps he was ashamed of it.

"Kent said you've spent the last few years trying to keep the town as untouched as when Brewster was alive, but you sound like you hate it."

Marc turned and looked directly at her. "I love it. But not as a memorial to the old man. I want to keep out the so-called trappings of civilization. I don't want to see it turned into a place for transient miners or a mecca for tourists with fast-food stands on every corner and people in shorts and sunglasses tossing their trash out car windows." The vehemence in his voice told Tracy a great deal. If he felt that strongly about tourists, imagine what he'd think about the gigantic earth movers carrying the ore out of the mountain. Kent was right. She had her work cut out for her. A chill of fear and uncertainty hit her.

Marc saw her shiver and said, "Come on. I have something else to show you."

Instead of returning the way they had come they followed what appeared to be a deeply rutted road leading up another canyon. The road ended, and again they had to maneuver around trees and boulders. At the top Marc stopped and pointed across a wide chasm to a spectacular mountain. Tracy had to look up to see the top, where a crown of ice rested on its granite head. No trees or shrubs softened the starkness of a scene made more ominous by the dark-gray clouds that hovered over it.

"That's where the richest supply of cobalt is. But to get to it that mountain would have to be destroyed. Do you have any concept of how destructive mining can be to a mountain, to streams?"

Seeing the beauty of the peak firsthand, experiencing its quiet magnificence, its awesome grandeur, was overpowering. Tracy stepped back, almost in fear, trying to lessen the feelings of her own insignificance. She had to look away from the dizzying height. Turning around so the mountain was behind her, she had a vision of what it would be like when the mining operation began. She could see the activity down on the valley floor where the base camp would be set up in preparation for the assault on the mountain. A road would pierce its sides, a pathway leading to the top of the mountain where its heart would be removed, leaving only a terrible scar. Tears filled her eyes. From deep within, one word came unbidden to her lips. "No!"

Without knowing how it happened, Tracy was suddenly in Marc's arms and he was whispering her name over and over again. He held her for a long time, sharing the moment with her.

Finally Tracy lifted her head from Marc's shoulder and they looked at each other.

"Tracy, you can see now why . . ."

"Marc." Tracy forced herself to sound calm, to get her emotions under control. "You've accomplished your purpose in bringing me here, but I have a question. Why did you send for a representative from Magnum?"

Marc's expression matched Tracy's. "Once a month I play poker at Mille Fleur. Elise sat in on one hand and bet me that if she won I'd at least listen to the sales pitch from Magnum." He shrugged. "I lost."

Tracy was too stunned to say anything. She turned away and walked toward her snowmobile, unwilling to have Marc see her reaction. Her worst fears had been realized. He had just been using her—her kisses, her body, her passion. He had never had any intention of seriously considering her sales pitch. What a fool she'd been. She had listened to her emotions and bungled the whole thing.

Anger suddenly flared. For the sake of her own self-respect, she was going to try. If he always won, as Elise had said, at least this time he'd get a good fight. And maybe . . . just maybe . . . Tracy turned and said, "Marc Durand, you have welshed on your bet."

A surprised look crossed Marc's face, an expression that quickly changed to alert wariness. "What do you mean?"

"You haven't heard the sales pitch from Magnum's representative. You haven't paid off the bet." Tracy's breath was clearly visible, and she realized that the day had turned much colder. "I want to leave your mountain and return to Mille Fleur House now. We'll read the proposal tonight."

Marc started to walk toward her, then stopped. He seemed to be contemplating what to do. He grinned. "OK, we'll go back. That will be better anyway."

Confused as to his meaning, Tracy started her engine and followed Marc. The trip to the red pickup truck took a long time. Once there, she helped load the snowmobiles and then gratefully climbed into the cab, too cold even to feel angry about what Marc had told her concerning the bet. What she needed was time away from him to get her perspective back. She had lost sight of her goals and needed to plan her next strategy. But later, not now. Cold, wet and hungry described her state. No junior executive could be expected to think under those circumstances. She shivered and wrapped her parka more tightly around her.

"Tracy, I'd be glad to show you my cure for frostbite again."

"No, thanks. I'll wait until it's been approved by the medical association." She leaned back and shut her eyes.

It was nearly dark by the time they stopped before the front door. Marc informed her that he'd be in after putting the snowmobiles away.

Just as Tracy climbed out of the truck, Marc's voice stopped her. "I've already shown you the best way to get warm. The next best is to take a hot shower. You'll find a robe and slippers you can wear in the closet. We'll have dinner when you're ready."

Tracy walked up the front path, inwardly expressing the hope that the bedroom and bathroom doors had locks. She found that they did and carefully secured them, wanting no more surprise visits. Even after a shower her cheeks felt tight from the cold and her eyes burned. The altitude, exercise and fresh air had made her sleepy, and she longed to lie down on the bed and take a nap. But hunger dictated that she quickly brush her hair loose, freshen her lipstick and find the robe Marc had mentioned. After examining the seductive Mandarin-style green silk with the slits up the sides she almost put on her still wet and muddy jeans. But the thought of her clean skin next to that clammy material made her shudder, and she slipped the sensual gown over her head. To whom did it belong? Elise? Or some other woman who had been charmed by Marc? The long gown brushed the floor. Whoever owned it was taller than Tracy . . . as Elise was.

When she opened the door, a mélange of odors—steaks and fresh-baked bread and cinnamon and apples—made her knees weak and her mouth water. She hurried toward the kitchen. Instead of Marc, however, she found a man tossing a Caesar salad, singing a country-western tune. The man's leatherlike skin was a map of wrinkles; his age could have been anywhere from fifty to eighty. Seeing Tracy, he stopped in midnote, turned and smiled.

"Marc's in the living room. I'm Harry Halliman. Hope you're hungry."

"Hello, Harry. I'm Tracy Cole. And yes, I'm starving."

"Good. It'll only be a few more minutes."

"Sure smells wonderful."

In the living room Tracy found Marc lighting the fire. When he saw her his eyes showed his admiration. "That robe suits you."

Marc, too, had showered and now wore a sport shirt and tailored wool slacks that emphasized his broad shoulders and narrow waist. Each time she was with him she saw something new that increased her awareness of him as a person. At first his handsomeness and the deviltry in his eyes had blinded her, and she had seen only one facet. But as Tracy learned more about the forces that drove him she discovered his maturity and power, and found that there were unknown depths to his character. Each new thing she learned added to her growing admiration for this man. And she didn't want to feel that way. What good would it do her, especially when he considered her purely as entertainment, someone to talk about at next month's poker game? Liking him could only lead to disappointment and heartache. Tracy didn't want to get into a stormy sea; she was looking for a safe, calm harbor.

Aware that she was staring, Tracy moved toward the polished-wood coffee table where two drinks sat on the tray. Marc stood and handed her one. "This is the third-best way to get warm." He smiled, a gesture that could easily make Tracy forget her quiet harbor. "Soon I'll run out of methods."

"I doubt that." Unwittingly, Tracy returned his smile. Sipping the bourbon and water, she sat on the swivel chair, again admiring the view outside, marveling at the gradations of blue and purple shadows that were cast on the snow. Swiveling her chair, she looked around the warm, comfortable room. The decorating touches, the pictures and lamps, the paperweight collection, all showed a woman's touch. Tracy wondered whose skill had made this room so inviting.

Harry soon called them to "come and get it." Tracy left her unfinished drink on the tray; fatigue, an empty stomach and whiskey were dangerous, and then to add Marc Durand . . .

Marc held her chair, and just as she sat down the phone rang. Harry answered it in the kitchen. He opened the door, leaned his head around the opening and said, "Tracy, a Jonathan Allen wants to talk to you." His voice dropped and he whispered, "He's been calling you all day. I forgot to tell you."

Tracy looked at the sizzling steak that nearly covered her plate, the baked potato, the salad with crisp lettuce and croutons, the fresh, hot rolls and said, "Tell him I'll call him later."

Marc laughed and said, "That's either a Magnum boss or a very close friend. I'm glad to see you have your priorities in the right order: food—then anything else.

Good for you." As he spoke he leaned over her shoulder to pour wine into her goblet.

Tracy waited impatiently until Marc was seated before she began to eat. Nothing had ever tasted so good. After a few minutes she stopped long enough to explain her call. "Jonathan Allen is my boss. He's probably calling to ask what's going on." Buttering a roll, she added, "I would like to tell him tonight that I have informed Mr. Marc Durand of the salient points of our deal and that he is seriously considering the matter."

Marc frowned. "Later." Then, to soften his gruffness, he added, "After dinner, I promise."

Forced to be satisfied with this concession, Tracy asked, "Do you have any brothers or sisters?"

"No, just me. Dad died three years ago. Gabrielle, my mother, spends the winters in Palm Springs for the sun, or San Francisco or New York for the theater. When she hears we had a lovely New Yorker visiting, she'll be sorry she left so soon." He poured more burgundy into Tracy's half-full glass. "You and she could have discussed the latest Broadway plays and musicals." He paused and added, "She'd like you." With the last words Marc's voice lowered, taking on a silky tone that conveyed some deeper meaning.

Tracy glanced away, suddenly embarrassed by the intensity of Marc's stare. Reaching for her wine, she said, "I would have enjoyed meeting her."

Perhaps by knowing Marc's mother Tracy could have painted a few more brush strokes on the slowly emerging portrait of Marc Durand.

After they had finished eating Harry came in and began to stack the plates. "It's snowing like hell. Sure is weird weather. Reminds me of the winter of '48. That one started in October, too. Snow eye-deep to a horse." He walked into the kitchen with the dishes. Still muttering about the weather, he returned and asked, "Coffee and dessert now or later?"

"Later, I think." Marc looked at Tracy, who readily agreed, too full to contemplate eating again for a long time.

"Then I'm going over to the bunkhouse. Everything's ready in the kitchen when you want it."

"That was a delicious meal, Harry. Thank you." Tracy folded her napkin and set it on the table. Harry seemed pleased by her compliment and rushed over to pull out her chair.

Marc took Tracy's arm, and they returned to the dimly lit living room; only one lamp and the glowing embers provided illumination. While Marc rebuilt the fire Tracy walked to the window. Beyond her own reflection was a world filled with swirling snow, the flakes madly dancing in the black night. Tracy refocused on her own image in the glass. Marc's face was beside hers. She hadn't heard him approach. Speaking without turning around, she said, "It's only 7:30, Marc. We could go to Mille Fleur House now, and I could show you the proposal." That damn proposal, that albatross around her neck.

"Yes, we could." He picked up a strand of hair and ran his fingers down the wavy length. Excitement prickled her skin. She wished Marc wouldn't stand so close, wouldn't touch her hair with such intimacy.

"Or you could verbally outline it for me here, and we wouldn't have to go out in the snow and cold."

"Yes, but would you listen?"

Marc laughed and tickled her cheek with the ends of a curl. "I always pay my gambling debts. I'll listen tonight, and then tomorrow I'll carefully read the entire contract. To show my good faith, Elise and Tom can join us, and together we'll go over the fine points . . . Tomorrow."

Tracy turned her back to the window and faced Marc. "Then let's begin the verbal presentation now."

He smiled but didn't move, examining her face as if memorizing it. He ran one finger along her cheek, then over her lips. Determined to keep her emotions in check, Tracy forced herself not to respond. Just as Marc began to bend his tall frame to kiss her she quickly moved aside, slipped past him and walked over to the swivel chair.

But Marc was faster, and he grabbed her arm, pulling her toward a dark-brown suede sofa. "If I have to listen you're not sitting across the room." He sat near her but didn't touch her. "OK, begin."

At last Tracy had an attentive Marc, seemingly ready and willing to listen to her. Now if she only knew what to say. How could she convince him to sell his beautiful mountain when she herself no longer believed it was the wisest thing to do? How could she minimize the terrible vision of what would happen if a mining operation came to Brewster? Yet this was what she had been trained to do. Persuading people that they wanted something they really didn't was why Magnum paid her a very good salary, why they had sent her here. Tracy suddenly felt very inadequate and ill-prepared.

"Marc, let me start by telling you that I'm not speaking as Tracy Cole but as the assistant director for acquisitions of Magnum Mining Corporation."

With these words her ambivalent position became clear. Tracy Cole, woman, wanted to keep Magnum from ever coming to Brewster. Tracy Cole, woman, wanted nothing to ruin the possibility that Marc might learn to think of her as a woman and not as a temporary playmate or business executive. And because of these feelings Tracy Cole, representative for Magnum, felt a disloyalty to her employer that deeply disturbed her. These discussions with Marc were going to be the most painful she had ever engaged in.

Marc said nothing, just watched her with interest, his body relaxed.

"What's the population of this area?" Tracy asked at last.

Marc seemed surprised by the abrupt question. "Brewster has about three hundred; the entire valley has about fifteen hundred. That's people, not cattle. Now, if we included livestock—"

Tracy interrupted. "And what was the population ten years ago?"

Marc's face grew serious. "About the same."

"Or a little higher?"

Marc shrugged, watching her with interest.

"And twenty years ago? Thirty years?"

Marc saw the direction of the questions, and his eyebrow rose, a sign this time of unwilling admiration.

"Right. The population has either remained the same or decreased. In demographics that's called zero growth. I call it stagnation, and it could lead Brewster into becoming another Patience."

Tracy twisted around so she faced Marc, pulling her knees up on the sofa. The slit on the side of her robe opened, revealing her tanned thigh and long bare leg. Marc's gaze shifted down.

"I like the sneak previews you give, Tracy."

Before he could say anything more Tracy pulled the robe closed. Marc grinned but returned his attention to her face, trying unsuccessfully to look serious.

"The young people of Brewster and this valley are not staying here to live," she said. "They go where they can find jobs. Unless they have a ranch to inherit or a business to take over they must leave to find a livelihood someplace else."

Tracy and the research department had done their homework well. Her confidence returned.

Next she explained that the students who did leave the area to seek work elsewhere left with a disadvantage. The scholastic scores of Brewster's high school students were slightly lower than the national average. The school system desperately needed more teachers, better facilities, more money. She reminded him of the narrow, poorly maintained county roads, how every year the frost further damaged the cement bridges and highways, how the community services for the young and the elderly had been cut.

Telling him things he probably already knew, she went on. "This area has one doctor—an aging man who wants to retire to Santa Barbara to be near his daughter. But he can't find anyone to buy his practice. People needing serious operations have to be flown to Pocatello or Boise, causing delays that have sometimes proved fatal."

"I see that more than geologists came to investigate our area. Your researchers did a thorough job." There was a cutting edge to his voice. He stood and went to the bar, returning with two half-filled brandy snifters. He handed one to Tracy and sat down again, this time closer to her. "And Magnum is miraculously going to solve all our social ills?"

Tracy thought about Marc's words while she swirled the amber liquid around in the glass, watching the way it clung to the sides like a veil of fine silk. She wondered how effective her arguments were. Was she swaying Marc, or was he only listening to her because of the bet? He was so damned unreadable, biting and sarcastic one minute, teasing and playful the next. Finally she spoke. "No, no miracles, but a modern, well-equipped clinic with a doctor and money coming into the area to help . . ."

"Ah, yes, money. That wonderful commodity that heals all wounds, solves all problems, eradicates all misery. But let's discuss the attendant side effects of money flowing into an area; let's . . ." Marc swallowed deeply of his brandy, set the glass down, turned toward Tracy and sighed, "Oh, hell, let's not."

His plaintive look, his somber, serious eyes, his surprising remark, all hit Tracy, and despite herself she laughed. The intense moment was broken.

With the change in mood a chill of anticipation swept over her. Marc took her glass, set it on the table and then slipped his arm around her body to draw her toward him. Tracy knew the opportunity to talk about the sale was lost, as were her well-rehearsed arguments. A mellowness came over her. She couldn't think anymore. Tomorrow . . . she'd think about it tomorrow when Marc came to town to read the contract, when she had her information before her in a businesslike setting and she was dressed in something that wasn't quite so conducive to seduction.

The silk of her gown rustled, a sensuous sound that sent a shiver up Tracy's spine. Was there an inevitability about what was happening? Did she have a choice? Did she want one? Where was the determination to make Marc stop seeing her as a temporary playmate? She forced herself to push away from Marc's arms, but as soon as he began to kiss her it was too late. The kiss started as a simple joining of their lips, a tender meeting to which Tracy tentatively responded, still unsure of what she wanted. Marc moved closer; his other hand touched her cheek and fanned out so that the tips of his fingers were buried in her thick hair. The kiss deepened and became a message center, telegraphing Marc's longing for her, his desire, his passion, his . . . love?

Since they had met Marc had thoroughly demonstrated that he wanted to make love to her. But could he be falling in love with her? Or was that just wishful thinking on her part?

Tracy's hand slipped behind Marc's neck; her other arm encircled his waist, holding him but making no commitment. Marc ended the kiss and looked deeply into Tracy's eyes. His own dark-blue ones were easy to read.

It was up to her. She must choose, and he would abide by her decision. Tracy knew that Marc had been leading her to this point ever since they had met. She had suspected all along that it would happen, and she honestly had to admit that she had secretly been anticipating it. This would be a special time, just as Friday evening had been. If she had nothing else, she would have two nights and a day filled with memories.

Determined to have this night at least, Tracy slipped out of Marc's arms, stood and reached for his hand, surprised at her own temerity. No words passed between them as Marc lifted and carried her, not to the room where she had changed earlier, but to what she assumed was his own. Tracy unwrapped one arm from around his neck and opened the door for them. Marc firmly swung it shut with his foot and deftly used his elbow to flip a wall switch that turned on a dresser lamp. While he walked toward the bed Tracy kicked off her slippers; they flew across the room, landing under a large chair.

Marc's lips found hers. He released her knees so that she slid down his body; she had to stand on tiptoe so her mouth wouldn't lose contact with his.

Finally the kiss ended; Marc's hands found the silk cord frogs that fastened the top of the robe and with difficulty slipped the knots out of their loops. He pulled the gown open and gazed at her, pleasure on his face.

"Ah, yes, that delightful bra of yours. I've been looking forward to this." He folded back the material from her shoulders, and she slid her arms out of the sleeves. The robe dropped to the floor; as Tracy stepped out of it Marc picked it up and laid it over a nearby chair. He must have seen a flicker of hesitation and doubt on Tracy's face, because he drew her close to him and whispered, "In case you're wondering, I bought that robe to give to my mother for her next birthday. It's not a prop in a seduction scene."

101

Tracy stepped back, still within the circle of his arms. "Marc, I'm an adult. I know what I'm doing. Besides, I'm getting used to your seduction scenes by now." Her brave words covered a growing uncertainty. Should she be here? Was she doing the right thing? She could see herself heading for that stormy sea. No quiet harbor ahead. But if she ever found that safe place she'd at least have this one night to remember. She reached out and, with as much care as he had shown, began to unbutton his shirt.

Marc looked surprised for a moment; then his hands dropped to his sides and he smiled, watching Tracy's every move. "What's good for the gander, huh, Tracy?"

Her hair had swung forward so that it partially covered her blushing face. "Hush, Marc. This is difficult . . . uh . . . standing here like this trying to . . . well, you see, I'm not . . . uh . . . not . . ."

Marc finished her sentence. ". . . not overly practiced in these matters." His voice lowered, taking on a seductive tone. "I know. A man can tell." With his index finger he lifted Tracy's head and looked into her eyes. His own were nearly black, and the teasing sparkle had disappeared.

"Let me teach you, Tracy. I took you to the mountain. Now let me take you on another trip that's even more full of wonder." He unsnapped her bra, and it fell to the floor. Again he gazed at her, his eyes showing his admiration for her body.

A breathless anticipation filled Tracy. She had made that commitment now. There was no backing out, not even if she wanted to. And with a joyous feeling, she realized she didn't want to. Her doubts vanished; she could take the journey with Marc. Stepping closer, she pulled the end of his belt from the loop and tried to unfasten the heavy leather. Marc didn't help, just stood there, a grin replacing his seriousness. Finally the belt was unfastened, and Tracy realized that it wasn't going to be easy being a liberated woman. Taking a deep breath, she unbuttoned the waistband and . . . stopped.

Marc laughed and pulled his shirt out of his slacks, slipped it off and tossed it on top of her robe. Tracy watched his movements as if mesmerized. Next came his shoes, socks and slacks. When he stood naked before her, Tracy, without any embarrassment, reached out and touched his broad chest, tanned to the color of burnished walnut.

"You're beautiful." The words escaped her thoughts, and Marc laughed.

"I'm supposed to say that about you." He placed his hands around her waist and drew her to him. "But instead of descriptive phrases, let me show you what I think of your body."

When Tracy's sensitive breasts touched the hair on Marc's chest, when their mouths met, an ache of desire began to grow that nothing could stop. Conscious only of her own longings, she was barely aware that Marc had released her, had slipped off her panties, holding her arm while she stepped out of them. He pulled back the bedspread, and Tracy lay on the cool sheets that smelled of sunshine. The lights were dimmed, and the room was filled with a soft golden glow.

Tracy tried to calm her racing heart by taking deep breaths, but she couldn't subdue her excitement, her anticipation, her growing desire. Suddenly he was beside her, and she gasped. At his touch she turned, eagerly accepting his body next to hers. Folding her in his arms, he sighed her name with his lips pressed to her temple. Then their mouths met in a frenzy of emotions and Tracy knew that Marc's feelings were as intense as her own. He began to kiss her eyes, her ears, her neck, her breasts, but returned often to her waiting mouth. With each kiss, with each touch of his hands as he explored her body, Tracy moved closer to the brink, prepared to fall into a labyrinth of unknown sensations.

Then Marc stopped and pulled away, looking at her body while his fingers caressed her breasts with feathery strokes. As if he were slowly running a car around an imaginary race track, he began to trace circles on her flat stomach. Tracy's ache for satisfaction increased. His slow careful touches, his unhurried pace, were driving her to the point where she had to do something or scream. With her own fingers she copied his actions, running her hands lightly over his hard abdomen, up his chest, touching the silken hair that hid his own nipples. She placed her mouth over one and nipped, teasing it with her tongue. Marc's quick intake of air told her what she wanted to know.

Marc gave a shaky sigh and said, "You really do believe that what's-good-for-the-goose stuff, don't you?"

"Yes, I do." She lifted one of his hands and kissed the palm, feeling the roughness with her lips. "I also believe that you're driving me crazy and . . ." Marc stopped her words with a hungry, demanding kiss that made her forget what she was going to say. His tongue encouraged hers to explore his mouth, where she tasted a sweetness more intoxicating than any wine.

So many sensations hit Tracy's brain at the same time that she slipped into a euphoric state from which she never wanted to return. She had to force her mind to sort out what was happening. First she concentrated on filling her lungs after Marc's devastating kiss. Then a burst of sensations hit her again when he cupped her breast in his large hand and placed his mouth on the mound, pulling at the nipple, rolling his tongue around it, causing a throbbing ache to explode deep inside her.

Tracy placed her hand on the back of Marc's neck, twining her fingers in his curly hair. No longer a rational, thinking being, she had become a creature who only responded to the incredibly exciting stimuli of Marc's body, Marc's hands, Marc's lips. The only intelligent thing Tracy could say came out as a low moan.

Placing both his hands on the sides of Tracy's head, Marc began to kiss her eyelashes, her nose, along her cheeks, her ears, and with each kiss Tracy silently said his name, repeating it over and over, turning it into a litany of one word. This whispered incantation was the last coherent thing Tracy remembered as Marc, with a fierce gentleness, continued his slow, systematic arousal of her passion.

Finally, just as she thought she would lose her sanity with the intensity of her feelings, she felt a deep shuddering, a series of tremors that shook her until she shouted his name, glorying in the ecstasy of the moment.

Slowly Tracy focused on the man who watched her with an unfathomable expression in his eyes. She lay back, coated with a sheen that made her skin resemble marble. Her breath still came in short, audible gasps. At last she could think more clearly and said his name in a question. "Marc?"

"Yes, Tracy." The communion between them was so complete that both knew that no words were necessary. Nothing could ever explain the chemistry of what had just happened to them.

Marc folded her in his arms and sighed, a sound of deep satisfaction. After a few minutes, Tracy spoke. "Marc, you know what just happened was *my* choice— not for nor on behalf of Magnum. You believe that, don't you?" Learning his answer was suddenly very important.

The silence that followed lasted long enough for Tracy to wonder if he could possibly not believe her. She drew back and looked at his enigmatic face.

"Marc, answer me!"

A smile erased his frown. He leaned forward and

kissed her mouth lightly, teasingly. "Of course I believe you, my lovely lady executive."

Tracy relaxed and molded herself against his warm body. She had been taut with fear, afraid to breathe until he had reassured her.

When her heart resumed its normal beat she said, "Marc, our Friday night together and this Sunday are special—a time apart. But tomorrow the lady executive returns, blue suit, white blouse, briefcase and all. I must present the proposal to you *tomorrow.*" She then added, "Agreed?"

"Well . . ." He bent down and placed his mouth on her breast, instantly bringing the nipple erect.

"Marc!" Tracy's first reaction was to push him away, but a stronger power forced her hands to the back of his head to keep his marvelous mouth there. Again a thundering ache rolled out of her core. She gasped as Marc led her to a new world of unimaginable delight and excitement. What she had felt before was a mere prelude to this journey, made all the more thrilling because Marc accompanied her as a full partner, sharing in the glory of the experience. When they both reached the height of passion Marc called her name and Tracy echoed it with his own. After a long throbbing fulfillment of their ecstasy, expressed simply by the whispering of their two names, they descended as they had climbed, together in body and spirit.

Afterward they lay quietly, lost in the remembrance of the exquisite moments. Their breathing returned to normal; their bodies cooled. Tracy had no idea how much time had passed. She sighed, not really caring.

A thought came, a new idea that intrigued her. A woman can love a man, let him make love to her, yet because of some code instilled in her, she feels she cannot declare that love until the man does. Why? Fear of rejection? Or is that from time immemorial men have taken the lead and women have found it difficult to be the aggressors in matters of love? Tracy knew that in this area the female population of the world still had a long way to go.

Then a new thought chilled her. Marc might not be falling in love with her. What if his attentions were to prove his original assumption, that Tracy had come here for one purpose: to use her body as an added bonus, a little inducement so he would be more willing to sell? What if his words had been a lie?

Tracy shivered, and tears filled her eyes. Marc reached down and covered them with a blanket, then drew her closer. "You're so silent. What's the matter?" He placed his hand under her chin, tilting her head so he could see her eyes. "Tears? Of sadness?"

With the back of his finger he caught a teardrop as it rolled down her cheek. He licked it off. Tracy turned and placed her hands on each side of his head. She'd analyze Marc and his philosophy later. Now she would savor their time together and hope it would never end.

"Or could they be tears of happiness?" Marc asked.

Drawing his mouth toward her, with her lips touching his, she whispered, "What do you think?"

7

The alarm clock rang, then stopped, rang and stopped, over and over. Tracy couldn't find the incessantly loud, on-again, off-again clock. She sat up and looked around. She was in Marc's bedroom. Turning to the other side of the large bed, she saw that she was alone. The bell rang again—not a clock, but the phone on a bedside table. Unsure if she should answer it, but willing to do anything to stop the noise, she reached for it and whispered, "Hello?"

Where was Marc? Had he slept at all? She didn't remember falling asleep.

"Hello. Hello? Who's there?" Tracy recognized the gruff voice of Jonathan Allen.

"Jonathan, this is Tracy." Of all the people in the world, the last person she wanted to talk to was her boss, especially this morning, when all she wanted to do was snuggle under the covers and remember. . . .

"What the hell's going on? I called all day yesterday and when I finally track you down, you say you'll call me back and—"

"Jon, calm yourself. I couldn't return your call."

Looking around the room, Tracy tried to find the clock. Spotting it on the dresser near the door, she squinted to read the time. Six-thirty! Of course, 8:30 in New York. When Jonathan Allen worked, he expected everyone else to be working, too, regardless of where they were. Then it hit her. Her boss had called her at 6:30 at Marc's house and who had answered? Tracy Cole, sounding thoroughly sleepy and . . . well, if sexual satiation could be communicated by voice, he'd have heard that, too. Oh, damn, why had she picked up the phone?

For the next half-hour Tracy tried to explain the delay in reporting her progress. Each sentence she said to Jonathan was an ambiguity or an equivocation, and some were outright prevarications. Why use fancy words? Tracy asked herself. She simply lied to Jonathan Allen, giving him an optimistic report that she knew was untrue. Marc had shown no sign of being willing to sell. His attitude could only be construed as negative. She should be preparing Jonathan for the worst, not soft-soaping the situation. But she couldn't tell him that Durand probably wouldn't sell his mountain and that she had failed in Brewster. Not yet, not until she was absolutely sure. . . .

While she talked Tracy tried to dress, but found it extremely difficult to hold onto the phone while putting on her bra and underpants and slipping the silk dress over her head. Finally Tracy said, "Jon, I really must hang up. We had a bad blizzard last night. Other people here need to use the phone." It was a poor excuse, but the only one she could think of. At least he'd think the house was full of snowbound people.

Before he could say anything more, she said, "Good-bye, Jon, I'll call you when I have something to report—good or bad."

Tracy looked in the mirror to check the state of her appearance. Not too bad, considering. She opened the door and looked down the hall. No sounds of activity in the house. Back in "her" room, she showered and put on her ski pants, which were still damp, but drier than and not as muddy as her jeans. She found herself wishing she had brought clothes for an overnight stay. But then . . . she hadn't known what was going to happen, had she? A faint blush pinked her cheeks when she remembered the events of the previous night. Forcing herself not to dwell on those exciting memories, she packed her wet clothes in her duffel bag and for the tenth time wondered where Marc was. Of course, this was a workday for him, and people started their activities early on a ranch. Surely he'd be outside, alone, she hoped. After slipping on her parka, she picked up her bags and walked out of the room and down the hall.

No one in the kitchen, no coffee brewing, no breakfast preparations. Harry Halliman must have other duties besides cooking. She opened the kitchen door and stepped outside. Sparkling snow lay on the ground in a foot-deep layer. Every twig and branch, every power line, every horizontal surface—all were perfectly coated with rounded mounds of snow. The storm had passed, leaving the sky fresh and clean, as if someone had thrown a bucket of blue paint on it. Footprints formed a path for her to follow through the snow. Nearby, she could hear the river murmuring as it dashed past the rocks.

The stable doors screeched as she opened them, drowning out her call for Marc. After the brightness outside, for a moment she could see nothing.

"Marc?" she called again.

"Miss Cole?" A man emerged from a stall, wiping his hands on a rag. It was Fred, the one who had saddled their horses that eternity ago—yesterday morning. Tracy tried to analyze the look he gave her, but saw only friendliness. No supercilious I-know-where-you-spent-the-night attitude. Still, embarrassment made her avoid eye contact.

"Marc left early to take hay out to the cattle. This storm caught us short-handed. I'm supposed to fix you something to eat and then drive you to town."

Disappointment hit her like a slap. Damn, she thought. He's vanished again. Marc was like the rabbit in a magician's hat—now you see him, now you don't. And today was to be Proposal Presentation Day. Was he avoiding the showdown? Then Tracy realized that the postponement might be for the best. In waiting, the still exciting memories of the night before would mellow. And the library at Mille Fleur House would be a setting more conducive to business than Marc's house.

"Thanks for the offer," Tracy said to the man, "but I'll eat at Mille Fleur House. Before I go, though, I would like to see the foal."

Fred switched on the overhead lights, and Tracy looked inside the stall. The mare stood patiently, pride in her offspring showing in her gentle eyes. Goblin's head was hidden underneath her as he nursed hungrily. "Goodbye, Goblin," she whispered. "I'll see you again, I hope."

Turning toward Fred, she said, "Could you drive me to town now? I'm ready."

"Sure thing, ma'am. I'll get the truck."

After leaving the ranch property they pulled onto the highway. While discussing the storm Tracy remembered her rental car and asked if this cold weather could damage the motor.

Fred shook his head. "Doubt it. It would have anti-freeze, and it's not that cold yet. It'll be fine. If you're worried about it, call Sam's Garage. He'll help you."

Without moving her head, Tracy took in the man's tanned, high-cheekboned face and wondered what he thought of the New York woman who had spent the night at Marc's house. Or was he so used to driving ladies home in the morning that he didn't give it a thought? Tracy turned and stared out the window, undecided whether she cared what Fred thought or not.

As Tracy climbed out of the truck a little while later, she said, "Thanks for the ride. Would you please ask Marc to call me as soon as he can?"

Back in her room, Tracy quickly stripped off her ski clothes and put on wool pants and a turtle-neck sweater. Since arriving in Brewster she had spent a great deal of time getting dressed and undressed and eating.

"And what did you do in Idaho, Tracy?" an imaginary interlocutor could ask.

"I changed my clothes innumerable times, ate like a glutton and fell in love. That's what I did in Idaho, Mr. Bones."

After that whimsical bit of dialogue Tracy wanted both to laugh and to cry. She had finally admitted that she did indeed love Marc. But what good was it going to do her?

Hardly aware of her action, Tracy sat down on a Queen Anne chair in front of the dressing table, a feeling of unhappiness washing over her. Love! It sure had a poor sense of place and timing. Not only was this the wrong place and the wrong time, but it was probably the wrong person, too. Nothing could come of it. Besides, she had her well-paying career in New York, she had her climb up the executive ladder, her apartment, friends, cultural activities. She had . . . what? Did any of them really matter?

Falling in love . . . the one thing the research department hadn't prepared her for. No fireworks, no flashing lights, no cannons booming in her head had warned her that it was coming. Falling in love had been such an unconscious act, more like a progression around a game board. Throw the dice, move forward three spaces; learn about Marc, see his strengths and weaknesses; five dots on the cubes, move to where her feelings changed from anger and frustration to respect; next turn, jump ahead to find that he was a gentle, caring lover. And then complete the circuit around the board, without any explosions or colored lights, to know she loved Marc.

She couldn't have told anyone exactly what love was. She only knew that whenever she was with him she felt an excitement she had never known before. Her heart beat faster; she was more sensitive, more aware, more alive, and she knew that she wanted to be with him constantly and forever.

She picked up her brush and ran the stiff bristles through her hair; the electricity made it crackle and form a halo of copper around her head. With each stroke of the brush, she reiterated her dilemma: She was in love with Marc Durand; they had had a wonder-filled night of sexual excitement that still made Tracy weak when she thought about it. Today she had to present the proposal, unsure if last night would make any difference; she knew she didn't want Magnum to come here and ruin Brewster, and the thought made her feel disloyal.

And, she asked herself, what about Elise? Could Marc be playing both sides of the street? Could he be planning on marrying Elise and still blithely having an affair with the naive Miss Cole, fresh from the big city, who had stupidly fallen in love with the handsome cowboy?

Now think, Tracy told herself. The only thing you have to go on is the talk of a town gossip. Has Marc shown any indication that he is at all interested in Elise? Judging by what she had seen he certainly hadn't. And yet . . . a little niggling doubt wouldn't go away.

Tracy suddenly felt a little ill; her head ached from the unanswered questions and her feelings of nervousness, fear and frustration. Rather than torture herself any longer she forced herself to finish dressing and went downstairs for some tea and toast.

Just as she walked out of the dining room, her stomach and head feeling better, Elise Schell entered the main hall. "Oh, Ms. Cole, I've been looking for you. Could you come meet my grandfather now? He's so much better in the morning."

Tracy wanted to dislike this woman, even though she knew it was unfair to pass judgment until she knew her better . . . and until after she discovered what the relationship between her and Marc was.

As they walked up the stairs Tracy told herself to go cautiously. Perhaps both Elise and Tracy were pawns in Marc's game. She said, "I'm sorry to hear that Mr. Schell has been ill. Is he improving?"

Today Elise looked especially lovely in a brown linen dress that emphasized her creamy skin. But if she lost another five pounds her fashionably slender figure would border on gaunt. She looked very tired. "Yes, thanks, he's always better after his treatment."

On the second floor they turned left; at the end of the hall they entered an overly warm room filled with bright sunshine. Sitting in a reclining chair near a large bay window was an old man, his still-handsome face wearing a welcoming smile.

"Hurry, Elise. Bring her in. I want to see this beautiful Tracy Cole I've heard so much about."

Mr. Schell must have the same sources as Kent Regan, Tracy thought. By now everyone in town had apparently discussed the new arrival from New York.

"How do you do, Mr. Schell?"

He took Tracy's hand in his, holding it while he said, "Well, Miss Cole, you're even better looking than I had heard." Turning toward Elise, he said, "Please bring that chair over here so our guest can sit near me. It's not often I can look at a redheaded beauty so close."

"I'll get some coffee for us," Elise said, placing a chair by the window. "Or would you prefer tea?"

"Tea, please," Tracy said and looked around the room which was filled with beautiful antiques. Mrs. Quartermain had been right. That "clever Elise" did have a flair for decorating.

Tracy relaxed and began to enjoy being flattered by the courtly Thomas Schell. For the next hour she answered questions about her background, her education, her interests and hobbies, her likes and dislikes. Usually reticent about herself, Tracy found that she liked talking to this man who showed such genuine interest in her. Elise said little, just sat and needlepointed a pillow in shades of pale yellow and pink.

Finally the conversation turned to Magnum and the reason Tracy was in Brewster. With slightly unsteady hands Thomas Schell set his cup and saucer on the tray and said, "Tracy, I want you to know my position on the sale of the mountain. I adamantly oppose it. Nothing you or Elise can say will change my mind."

Surprised at his bluntness, Tracy looked over at Elise, who had stopped embroidering and now watched the two of them.

"Mr. Schell, as I understand the situation, Elise and Marc Durand are the two legal owners. You have turned over all rights of ownership to Elise. Is that correct?"

Thomas Schell sighed. "Yes. I just didn't think she'd sell it, that's all." He leaned his head on the back of the chair, suddenly looking much older. "But she must do what she feels is right." Looking toward his granddaughter, he said, "Elise, I must excuse myself and leave our beautiful guest. I'm very tired."

With Elise's help he stood. Pulling back his shoulders so he stood taller, he said, "Tracy Cole, I know you'll be fair. Meeting you has been a pleasure."

She reached out to take his hand and said, "I hope to see you again before I leave, Mr. Schell. I enjoyed meeting you very much."

When Elise returned from the bedroom she opened one of the windows, letting in a cool breeze that Tracy welcomed.

"Grandpa makes me keep this room at eighty degrees. I about suffocate." She sat down and continued working on the nearly finished pillow. "I hope you didn't mind all of his questions. He gets lonely."

"Not at all. I liked your grandfather. I just hope my visit didn't exhaust him too much."

Elise reached for her scissors and cut a strand of wool. "He'll be fine after a nap." She paused and said, "You must think I'm an avaricious ingrate to want to sell that land against my grandfather's wishes."

"I'm not here to pass judgment on your actions. My job is to negotiate the sale."

"Let me explain my position." She looked out the window for a moment. "And please keep what I have to say to yourself."

Tracy nodded her agreement.

"Running Mille Fleur House takes all our cash, and I've borrowed as much as I can. Grandpa doesn't know there isn't any money." She sighed. "Besides my grandfather and myself, my husband's mother lives here, as does Mrs. Quartermain. She's been our housekeeper for years and is supposed to be retired. In exchange for room and board she stays to help. I couldn't have managed without her."

Elise picked up her embroidery needle and poked it in the arm of her chair, making a circle of dots in the material.

"Then there are Grandpa's unbelievable medical costs. He has to go to Seattle for treatment every four weeks. If he knew the financial situation he'd refuse to go."

And, Tracy thought, Marc flies him there to save the

cost of transportation. Piece by piece, the picture in the jigsaw puzzle was being revealed.

"Turning the solarium into a restaurant and opening a cocktail lounge have helped some. But the guest rooms bring in very little. Not many people come here to stay."

So, Tracy thought, that's why the dining room was crowded, even on Saturday and Sunday. The people of the community were trying to help, too.

Elise suddenly began to busy herself with her stitches, not looking at Tracy. "Sorry about boring you with my sob story. But I wanted you to see my side of it."

"Wasn't there any insurance after your husband's death?"

Elise looked up, a flash of hatred in her eyes. "Insurance? That's the best joke of all. You see, I was married to Frank for eight years. Out of that, we had three good ones. Five years ago, about the same time that Abigail, Marc's wife, left Idaho, Frank changed. We started to fight—about money, about everything—but especially about Marc Durand. Frank became insanely jealous, accusing me of being in love with Marc, of having an affair with him."

Elise's head was bowed, and Tracy could see how difficult it was for her to tell this story. The light from the window shone on her hair, making it look almost silver. After a long silence Elise again spoke.

"We'd separate, then there'd be a reconciliation. But the pattern would begin all over again." She looked up. "When he drank . . . those were the bad times." Her gaze fell to her hands. "In the end Frank got the ultimate revenge. He had an insurance policy that would have paid if he had lived one more week. But the court ruled that his death was suicide, and the insurance company wouldn't pay."

"What do you mean? Lived one more week?"

"Insurance policies are void if a suicide occurs within two years of their issue date. Frank's death came one week too early."

"Oh, I'm so sorry."

Elise looked up. No tears clouded her eyes. "I don't mind talking about it now. I just wanted you to see how important this sale is to me." She straightened her shoulders and took a deep breath, as if she had found a new strength. "I don't want Grandpa and Mrs. Harlow and Mrs. Quartermain to have to go into a home for the elderly." A fierceness came into her eyes, making her look more animated, more alive. "And I don't want this lovely old house destroyed by neglect. It's been in my family since my great-grandfather married a Brewster. That mountain is useless to me. We need the money, not the land."

Nothing is ever simple, Tracy thought. Destroy a wilderness area and save a 100-year-old mansion. What a choice.

"And in the new poker game, with you and Marc again as the players, he holds the winning hand. You can't sell unless he agrees."

Elise looked up in surprise. "He told you about our bet?"

"Well, not willingly." A vision of the mountain with its overwhelming beauty flashed in Tracy's mind. She remembered how deeply moved she had been, how Marc, with gentleness and empathy, had held her in his arms and how the moment had been shattered by Marc's admission of why he had sent for a representative. Slowly Tracy refocused on the woman sitting across from her.

For the first time Elise was smiling; it changed her face dramatically, making her look younger, almost carefree. "Good for you. Marc needs someone to stand up to him once in a while. He's entirely too arrogant."

A tentative knock at the door interrupted them. Elise

muttered a quiet "damn" and then said, "That's my mother-in-law, Mrs. Harlow. She's a little senile and very deaf. You won't hurt my feelings if you leave. I have to get her snack."

"Thanks. I really should leave anyway. I want to go to the town square. With this new snow, it will be lovely." Tracy stood to go.

Elise opened the door, but instead of letting the minuscule woman in, she took her by the arm and, after Tracy entered the corridor, she shut the door. "I won't introduce you. She couldn't hear me and wouldn't remember anyway. I'll take her back to her room."

Reaching out for Tracy's hand, she said, "Come again. And please let me know what happens with Marc." She smiled and added, "Good luck. You'll need it." She led Mrs. Harlow down the hall.

As Tracy watched the slender woman walk away she suddenly knew that she liked and respected Elise Schell and desperately hoped she could help—somehow.

After the Schells' too-warm apartment, the crisp outside air felt good. Tracy breathed in deeply, savoring the scent of pine and sage and sunshine. In the western sky chalky gray clouds ominously obscured the upper peaks of the mountains. Soon the sun would also be enfolded in that wrapping of sheep's wool. As Tracy walked toward the square she remembered the last time she had been that way. Had it been only Saturday? Had just two days passed? So much had happened. . . .

As she neared the square Tracy realized that she still faced the same dilemma as she had when she had first seen this unique town, only now her problem was compounded by her changed position with Marc. And the trouble was she had no one with whom to discuss it, no one to whom she could turn. . . . Yes, there was someone. Kent Regan. Perhaps he could help. She searched the streets that bordered the square until she found the bank, then hurried her steps toward the glass-fronted building with BREWSTER TIMES printed in gold on the window. A bell above the door jangled merrily, but no one came to the long counter that divided the room. Tracy noticed the not unpleasant odor of printing ink combined with the surprising aromas of coffee and bacon.

On the walls of the room were large frames holding yellowed newspapers, their headlines proclaiming important events: TOBIAS BREWSTER DEAD AT 93. ARMISTICE AT LAST. STOCK MARKET CRASHES. PEARL HARBOR ATTACKED.

"Tracy?" She turned to see Kent standing by a door near the back of the long room. He was drying his hands on a dish towel tied around his waist.

"Come on back. You've missed breakfast, but we'll have coffee, then I'll give you your tour."

Tracy slipped through a narrow opening in the counter, walked around a huge printing press that looked like one Benjamin Franklin could have used and entered a small storage area. To the right was a staircase where Kent waited. "I live up here on the nights I have to put out the paper. I'm glad you've come."

Upstairs the large room had been converted into an apartment. The walls were lined with books, and one section held fishing rods, reels and feathery tied flies.

Kent poured two cups of coffee and led her to the upholstered chairs that were placed before a potbellied stove in the middle of the room. Feeling relaxed and at ease with this man who had been a stranger twenty-four hours ago, Tracy waited for Kent to speak.

"Well, Tracy, what do you think of Brewster?"

She told him of her surprise and delight. "And that's my problem. I think more and more about the negative effects that a mining operation would have on this area and find it increasingly difficult to think of the benefits. I know all the antimining arguments Marc will use on me because I've used them all on myself a hundred times since I saw the town and the mountain."

Kent didn't speak, just filled his pipe carefully, as if it were the most delicate of operations.

"I've never faced this problem before." Tracy whispered the words, revealing the depth of her feelings.

"It sounds like you're torn between loyalty to your employer and your growing love for this area."

And my growing love for Marc Durand, Tracy silently added. That problem might be the most difficult one to solve.

Kent started the ritual of lighting his pipe. "I can't advise you. This is something you'll have to work out for yourself."

"Yes, I know. One minute I think I know which way to go, and then I hear Elise's reasons for wanting to sell, and another weight goes on that side of the scale."

"You've talked to Elise?" He held the match an inch from the bowl of the pipe.

"Yes, this morning. I met Mr. Schell, too. He's against selling."

Kent puffed on his pipe until smoke wreathed his blond head. "Yes, I know. But he doesn't understand the financial situation and Elise refuses to tell him." Another aromatic cloud drifted toward the stove. "She hopes that selling the land will solve all her problems. But Marc holds the key, and he'll do what he thinks best."

Tracy looked down at the braided rug lying under their feet and said, "Implicit in your comment is the belief that Marc won't sell anyway, so I'm wasting my time."

"No, I didn't say that."

"Kent, I know about the bet and why I was sent for. But I keep thinking that if I can ever tell him the advantages, and there are many, perhaps he'll reconsider. The Schells' position, the medical clinic, keeping the young people here so the town doesn't die, the increased revenue to help the area . . . all these should make him want to have a mine here."

"Marc will listen to everything you have to say, weigh all the positive and negative factors and take into consideration Elise's predicament. Then he'll come to a decision. And only he knows what that will be. He has a lot of pressures on him that make his position difficult. I don't know what I'd do in his place."

"If Elise can't sell the land, what will *she* do? What will happen to her grandfather and Mrs. Harlow and Mille Fleur House?"

"Elise will find a way. She's a very determined woman and a fighter. She'll make it."

"Kent, I have to ask. What's the relationship between her and Marc?"

"Well . . ." The phone's harsh ring interrupted him. "Excuse me."

He went to the massive desk and picked up the receiver. "Hello?"

Tracy stood and walked to the window. In the square a child was pulling a huge sled, heading for a small hill behind the bandstand. What was Kent going to say? Tracy asked herself. She felt as frustrated as the child below, who was trying to maneuver his too-big sled up the hill.

"Yes," Kent said. Pause. "No." Another longer pause. "Soon, I think . . . OK, I'll tell her. 'Bye."

Tracy turned as Kent approached. "That was Marc. He's looking for you. Says something about a 'damn unpaid debt' or words to that effect. He'll meet you at Mille Fleur in a half-hour."

At last, after waiting three days, Marc had finally agreed to listen. But she had only half an hour to get ready for the big meeting. She'd have to postpone getting Kent's answer.

"I'd better go. Thanks for listening, Kent." She held out her hand, and he took it in his own large ones.

He smiled at her. "We have a saying in Idaho: 'Great works are performed not by strength but by perseverance.'"

Tracy thought for a minute, then smiled. "Sounds like something you found in a fortune cookie."

"Samuel Johnson. Here's another: 'Winning can be losing.'"

Tracy reached for her parka and laughed. "Now that's a cryptic remark. Care to explain?" They walked down the stairs. At the front door Kent said, "You think about my hometown homilies. Winners can end up with nothing. Come back for the tour and good luck, you'll—"

Tracy interrupted. "Don't say it. I know, I'll need it. Thanks for the advice."

She waved at him as she waited at the corner for a car to pass, then, with hurried steps, headed toward the inn.

8

⛓⛓⛓⛓⛓⛓⛓⛓⛓

After entering Mille Fleur House she ran up the stairs, determined to be ready and waiting in the library when Marc arrived. Her hands shook as she inserted the ornate skeleton key into the lock. As soon as she was inside she pulled off the sweater and slacks and brushed her hair, twisting it into a bun at the back of her head. To diminish the severity of the hair style she let a few tendrils escape at the sides of her face. Eyebrows were smoothed, eye shadow and lipstick freshened. Her cheeks glowed with a natural blush that made her changeable green eyes look luminous. After pulling on nylons she stepped into a slightly flared navy-blue wool skirt. The matching jacket had diagonal stitching to add interest to the straight-cut design. A severely tailored long-sleeved silk blouse that buttoned high at the neck, a Victorian gold bracelet and dark-blue sling pumps completed the outfit. Tracy took a last look at herself and, remembering the final touch, slipped on the glasses she liked to wear for reading. Their frames added just the perfect touch for the uniform of a lady executive, junior grade.

Ready at last, Tracy found her briefcase and handbag

and left the room to look for Mrs. Quartermain. After a frantic search throughout the entire building, from attic to furnace room, Tracy found the housekeeper in a storage area sitting on a cardboard box checking cans of pineapple juice.

"Oh, Tracy, I was looking for you last night. Did that man who called you all day yesterday finally find you? He attacked our efficiency here in Idaho, said we didn't know our head from a teakettle, or something like that. I told him—"

"I'm sorry, Mrs. Quartermain. Jonathan Allen can be a little unreasonable when he doesn't get immediate gratification." Tracy reached out to help the woman to her feet. "I need to use the library. I'm meeting Marc Durand in about five minutes and—"

"But the fire's not lit, and the radiators are turned off. It'll be cold and musty. You should have warned me. My goodness, people can't—"

Following their pattern of interrupting each other, Tracy said, "That's OK. I'll light the fire; it won't take long to warm the room. Please?"

"Well, I really must finish this inventory. I guess Elise won't mind if I just give you the key."

Tracy nervously grabbed it, turned and hurried up the stairs, shouting her thanks back to the confused Mrs. Quartermain.

Stopping by the dining room, Tracy left a message with the hostess, telling Marc where to find her. The library, on the opposite side of the building from the Schells' apartment, was indeed cold and smelled of old paper and leather. The paneled walls were lined with shelves holding hundreds of books, giving the room a stately, quiet appearance. A ladder attached to a runner could circle the room to give access to the top shelves.

The fire was all laid, ready for a match, which she quickly applied. The large room had lots of furniture

grouped into conversation areas, like islands. Forming a
"U" around the fireplace were two wing-back chairs that
faced each other with a velvet-covered sofa between
them. With difficulty Tracy pushed the sofa back. This
way Marc would be forced to sit in the much safer chair.
She wanted nothing to distract his attention.

After shoving the two chairs closer to the now crackling
fire, she lit the nearby table lamps, flooding the area with
a circle of light that looked inviting and . . . intimate?
Perhaps this was the wrong setting. Should she sit at the
desk that sat over by the window, with Marc opposite her
like an employee called in to talk to the boss? No, this was
better. She didn't want to overdo the representative-
versus-seller bit.

Sitting down in her chair, she glanced at her watch and
realized that it was lunchtime. Marc was late; perhaps he
had stopped to eat. Or would he try another delaying
tactic by ordering food to be served up here? Tracy
remembered that he had said the Schells could be
present during the discussion. But she wanted to lay all
the facts out for him without the distraction of other
people and decided not to call them. Convincing Marc
was her primary objective now.

Tracy pulled a small inlaid table close to her chair,
opened her briefcase, extracted the thick folders and
reimmersed herself in the dry, technical language of the
preliminary environmental-impact studies. But she didn't
see the words on the printed page. In her mind she could
hear Kent's last remark: "Winning can be losing." Winning what? *Losing* what? And the phone had interrupted
him just as he was going to explain about Elise and Marc.

Shaking her head in frustration, she again tried to
concentrate. There was so much material, so many facts
to present to Marc to prove that Magnum's coming here
would not be entirely detrimental. But her mind refused
to do her bidding, and the image changed to the one she

had been avoiding for hours . . . the remembrance of the wonder of the night before, when their two bodies had joined and become one . . . the remembrance of Marc taking her to a world of sensual pleasures that still brought back a throbbing ache. Leaning her head on the back of the chair, she closed her eyes, and the painting on the back of her lids was of their bodies intimately entwined, his own darkly tanned skin a contrast to her paler complexion, of Marc slowly, patiently using his hands, his lips, his body to awaken her slumbering passion, of Marc teaching her how to use her own body to give him pleasure and of how, together, they had created a special time that would forever be locked in her mind. She could still feel the sensation of him stroking her, running his hands over the dips and curves of her naked body, his murmuring voice telling her of her beauty, his laughter when he found an odd-shaped birthmark that few people had ever seen. . . .

In her thoughts she could hear Marc call her name as he had done when they had both been filled with the ecstasy of desire. "Tracy?" his voice said, and she answered, "Yes, Marc."

In her dream his lips met hers in a phantom kiss that set her heart racing; she saw herself reach up to pull him closer, wanting to deepen the contact, wanting to feel his lips bruise hers with his commanding desire. When Tracy's hands touched something rough and warm her eyes flew open. Bending in front of her, his hands on the chair arms, was Marc, so close that his face was blurred. Before she could react he took off her glasses, tossing them carelessly on the table. His lips again found hers and, with a hard insistence, forced her to respond.

Lost for a moment in the unbearable pleasure of his kiss, now that she knew it wasn't a dream, Tracy gave what Marc demanded. But when he stopped to pull her out of her chair reality returned. He had done it again, this time with a sneak attack, but the results were the same. His kisses made everything disappear, all her resolve and new-found strength, all her carefully made plans.

"Marc," she whispered, "please don't . . ." But Tracy was already on her feet, her body wrapped in Marc's arms, his head coming down, again seeking her lips. As much as she wanted to yield to him, she forced herself to remain rigid, communicating in the only way she could that she was no longer going to let physical desires rule her mind. Just as Marc was about to kiss her she moved her head and his mouth brushed her cheek.

"Damn it, Tracy, hold still." He placed his hand on the back of her head while he gazed down at her. She tried unsuccessfully to turn her face from his searching eyes and his hold tightened.

"So, you don't want to kiss me? Well, I think you do. If I remember correctly, you're particularly susceptible to being touched here. . . ." He lightly brushed her breast. Tracy gasped. As if a switch had been turned on, all the emotions and sensations she had experienced the night before returned, and she longed to have him draw her to him, to have him . . . No! That was just what he wanted, to dominate her physically. She was back on the same merry-go-round as before.

"Marc! Let me go!" She tried to force him to release her. In answer to her demand he held her tighter, running his hand under her jacket, touching her through the thin blouse.

"Tracy, you were sitting here in this library, dreaming of me, remembering last night."

Tracy shook her head and fought against his strength to be set free.

"Oh, yes, you were. You even spoke my name aloud, and when I kissed you, you responded. You can't deny that." His voice deepened with emotion. "Tracy, what we had last night was an incredible experience. Do you have any idea how wonderful and rare it was? How can you expect me just to forget how absolutely perfect we were together?" Still holding her with one hand, Marc put his other at her neck, slipping the top button from its slot. "How can you deny me the right to take off this prim blouse and your bra so I can press my lips to your lovely breasts again? How can you expect me to keep my hands off you?" Marc's smoky eyes changed to a deep blue, desire plain in them. "Tracy, if you knew how long I watched you sleeping in my arms, how I wanted to rouse you from your sleep and reawaken your passion . . ." Marc's voice was low, filled with an intensity that shook Tracy. "I've been in agony all morning, waiting until I could come to you, needing you, wanting you. . . ."

While Marc spoke his language of sensual desire Tracy waited for the one word she had to hear. He talked of wanting her, needing her, but only to make love. There was no mention of *loving* her.

Well, what had she expected? She was undoubtedly just a weekend fling for Marc. But she had wanted more than that, had desperately hoped for . . . well, if not a commitment, at least the possibility of one. Anything to take away the pain of emptiness and doubt that threatened to engulf her. Perhaps if she had more time, or if they had met under different circumstances, where she and Marc weren't on opposite sides . . . But they were, and the showdown had been delayed too long. She never should have allowed Marc to make love to her. Now the words she must say were the most difficult ones she had ever had to utter.

Marc was just bending down to capture her lips with his when Tracy spoke. "Marc, please listen to me." She leaned back to see his face better. "I . . ." She stopped and swallowed, then began again. "I told you that last night was a special time . . ." She didn't dare add how exquisite that time had been. "But I also said that the lady executive would return today. We have to discuss Magnum *now*."

Marc's frown returned. Tracy could see the desire in his eyes change to anger and frustration. Good, Tracy thought, now he could experience the same emotions that had plagued her for days.

"Tracy, I . . ." He took a deep breath and let it out in a sigh of resignation. Perhaps he, too, hated to draw the battle lines, hated their being on opposite sides. "OK, I'll listen to your presentation, and I'll even keep an open mind. But before we start, we have some unfinished business to take care of."

In a movement that took Tracy's breath away he took her arms and placed them around his neck, pressing her body to his and lifting her up so her feet were off the floor. He bent his head and reconfirmed the passion that had overcome her the night before.

But suddenly Tracy found herself standing alone. Marc no longer held her against him. Opening her eyes, she blinked in surprise and took a deep, shuddering breath, waiting for Marc to speak.

"There. Now, let's take a look at you." He walked around her, seemingly cool and in control, examining her from the coiled hair on top of her head down to her slender feet.

"Well, so this is the uniform. My, my, it really is something." His voice was cool and calm, belying his earlier emotional state. He picked up her glasses from the table. "Here. I think these are *de rigueur*." He slipped them over her ears, pushing them up the bridge of her nose. "Now, you are the very modern model of a junior executive, type HSF, class 1-A."

"HSF?" Tracy asked coldly, determined to prevent Marc from knowing how upset she was.

"That's the newest prototype, *Homo sapiens:* female, and I can say from experience that you are definitely class 1-A."

Tracy wanted to end this conversation now. Turning quickly away, she walked to her chair, sat down, yanked the folders onto her lap and looked up at Marc, who stood watching her, his arms crossed.

"Why don't you put another log on the fire, Marc? The room is still chilly."

"It's not the only thing that's cold around here," he said, complying with her request.

At last he sat facing her. He had showered, his hair was still damp and he wore clean jeans and a creamy Aran Isle sweater. "Well, Ms. Cole, now that we've dispensed with the preliminaries, what does the assistant director for acquisitions have to say to me?" He looked around, inspecting their surroundings. "You've set the scene very carefully. Sofa pushed back from the fire. Two chairs facing each other, you in one, me in the other. Too bad you had to ruin the effect by falling asleep . . . perchance to dream."

Damn the man, Tracy thought, he was a consummate actor, changing from emotion-filled words to sarcastic quotes from Shakespeare. Looking down at the folders, she went through them until she found the two thickest ones. Setting the others aside she forced herself to match his coolness. He wouldn't goad her into any battle of words.

Handing Marc one folder, she said, "Here's a summary of the preliminary socioeconomic-impact report and the environmental studies that Magnum prepared. They were done by an independent research firm approved by the United States Forest Service." She opened her own copy, turning the pages until she said, "If you'll begin on page three and read to page seven, you'll see in capsule form the company's plans for the area."

"OK, Ms. Junior Executive, I'll do as you ask . . . for now." He relaxed and began to read.

Tracy leaned back in her chair and watched him. Despite his lanky frame, he looked at ease and comfortable in the wing-back chair. His legs were crossed, and the faded blue denim of his jeans was molded to thighs that Tracy knew were tanned and muscled. Turning her thoughts away from Marc's physical attributes, she remembered how he had found her here, a spider waiting for the fly, asleep in the parlor. But the hunter had got caught by the prey.

How could she have been so stupid as to sit with her eyes closed, dreaming of him, wanting him, reliving those pleasure-filled moments? Afraid that Marc would look over and read the unhappiness in her eyes, Tracy turned her gaze toward the fireplace to watch the flames twirl and pirouette, dip and sway to the fire's own music. She had left herself wide open to his advances. How he must have enjoyed finding her here, smoldering with excitement from her memories, needing only his lips to touch hers for her passion to ignite.

". . . you assigned." Marc's voice finally penetrated her thoughts.

"What did you say?"

"I'll repeat it for the third time. I said that I've finished reading the pages you assigned." He wore a faint smile, and one eyebrow was raised. Tracy knew that all the emotions she had been reexperiencing showed on her face.

"Are you still dreaming about last night?" His voice was now pitched low and had that familiar seductive quality that sent chills up Tracy's spine and made her face redden. Twice he had caught her off guard. She *must* keep her mind on her business.

"No, I wasn't. I was thinking of the benefits Magnum could provide for Brewster."

Marc laughed, a sound that filled the quiet room. "You're fantastic, Tracy. When you get caught thinking erotic thoughts, you blush so beautifully and lie without blinking an eye."

The room had grown too warm; Tracy took off her glasses and set them on the table, then leaned forward to slip off her jacket, laying it over the arm of the chair. As she opened the top buttons of her constricting blouse she glanced at Marc. Amused interest made his eyes sparkle; he wouldn't let this opportunity pass without saying something suggestive.

"You're really preparing for battle, aren't you? But what kind of war? If you keep unbuttoning that blouse your opponent is liable to get the wrong impression."

Tracy ignored him; she must communicate to him that the time for fun and games was over. "Marc, do you have any idea how extremely important cobalt is?" Without waiting for his answer she continued. "The United States is crucially dependent upon foreign sources for twenty-two nonfuel minerals. Political instability in certain countries has forced our government to try to decrease our dependence on importing these metals."

A log shifted, and a storm of sparks scattered up the flue. Tracy wished she had thought to bring up a carafe of water. "Cobalt is essential to jet engines, nuclear-propulsion systems, high-speed cutting tools, synthetic-fuel production. With any high-grade steel subject to extreme heat, cobalt is vital. If other sources aren't found, it could be the oil embargo all over again, with the U.S. caught holding the short end of the stick. Only 42 percent of our oil is imported. We import 93 percent of our cobalt." She paused to allow Marc to speak. He sat silently, observing her with an unreadable expression on his face.

Finally Marc sighed, turned his gaze toward the fire and spoke, almost as if he were thinking aloud. "What a strange sequence of events. The leading source of cobalt is the Shaba Province in Zaire, Africa. In 1978, Cuban-trained troops invade the district and disrupt the mining. The price skyrockets, the U.S. panics and mining companies start looking for other sources. And they find Brewster, just waiting to be exploited. So now, years later, here you are."

Yes, thought Tracy, that little war in a far-off country had led her to this mansion in the middle of Idaho, facing a man she had grown to love, asking him to give up something *he* loved.

"What do you think of the information in the report?"

Marc looked relaxed, but she could see a tenseness about him that proved he was working hard at keeping his emotions in check.

"It's clear and concise. It gives statistics to back up what you said last night. But you didn't tell me that over the next five years, eleven hundred people would be employed. That seems extremely high."

"They'll need about five hundred for the twenty-four-hour mining and milling operations. The other six hundred will be service personnel, office employees, construction workers." Tracy described the crushing, milling and storage facilities that would be built. Now she was doing what she had been trained for. No more dreams, doubts or questions . . . at least not for now.

"Where would these projects be?"

"Possibly in that valley where we parked the pickup. The crushing mill would probably be at the base of the mountain." Tracy thought of those lovely places, so untouched by man. The full realization of what she was asking Marc to give up hit her. How utterly callous and insensitive she must sound, to state unemotionally that the crushing mill would be situated in that pine- and aspen-filled glen, which was now so quiet and peaceful, home to thousands of small animals and birds. She longed to tell him how the image of that noisy, dusty, ugly, utilitarian building in that beautiful place made her physically ill.

Marc nodded and said, "And I see that 45 percent of the permanent jobs would be filled by local people with an annual payroll of over $15 million."

"Yes, Magnum has a complete training program. It's a marvelous opportunity for the young people—"

Marc interrupted. "Oh, yes, as long as they want to work at hard-rock mining in deep holes in the earth." He spoke the words with little inflection, but his cynicism was obvious.

"But the young people would stay here and become a vital part of the town."

Marc's face showed his growing fury, and his next words were harsh and cutting. "That all sounds good, Tracy, but those people staying here would be trained to work at jobs that might end at any time. When the mine closed they'd have to move to find other work."

"Magnum has planned for the operation to last at least fifteen years. In mining, that's a long time. Forty million dollars wouldn't be spent on a project that would quickly fold. Also, there would be a tax-prepayment program to help the county and the school districts with capital improvements—new school facilities, a well-equipped clinic with physicians. And nearly half of that payroll of $15 million would be disposable income—spent locally to make Brewster a growing community."

"My God," Marc said, "that kind of payroll would

mean millions of dollars coming into Brewster each year. Fast-food restaurants, stores, bars would spring up so all those wage earners could spend all that money."

"But with a strong county government, zoning laws could be instituted. Money coming into an area doesn't necessarily mean instant urban blight."

"Then why are so many towns in the United States utterly lacking in charm? Zoning laws tend to be changed to favor whoever has the most cash." He sighed and stretched his legs out in front of him, as if weary of this discussion.

"Tell me about the type of mining that would be done," he said. "I think it used to be called rape-ruin-and-run mining. What's the name for it now?"

Tracy felt surprisingly angry at his words. Despite her misgivings about the wisdom of Magnum coming, she felt a loyalty toward the company. His condemnation was unfair and unjustified. Magnum didn't operate that way; the environmental-protection laws as well as company policy made sure of that. Determined not to let him goad her into losing her temper, she answered with cold civility. "Rape-ruin-and-run mining, as you call it, is no longer the method, nor would strip mining be done here. Magnum would use cut-and-fill mining."

He sat up. "Yes. But that means another area has to be stripped to fill in for the displaced ore. Somewhere along the line, a mountain would be destroyed."

"Millions of dollars would be spent to minimize the adverse effects on the environment. The wildlife would be protected; reforestation would be a continuing process. Only reclaimed clean water would be released into the streams. The kind of mining that was done in Tobias Brewster's time is no longer allowed. There are protection agencies and permits and regulations that would make Brewster throw up his hands and return to Massachusetts and take up farming."

"Tracy, you're so good at spouting the company line."
He leaned back in his chair and ran his hand through his
hair, ruffling the dark curls. "Let's say that Magnum can
keep the damage down to a minimum and that when
they leave, they restore the land to its former beauty."
He leaned forward, setting his arms on his knees, staring
directly into her eyes. "But think about the impact on
Brewster and this whole area. Think about the trailer
cities that grow up around mining towns. I mentioned the
fast-food places and the bars before. Nothing has been
said about the single men who would come to work the
mines. What entertainment would they have in a community where the family unit is so important? Drinking
and bar hopping? And what about the women who
make their living off men? They're sure to come. I've
seen how the shale-oil operations have turned sleepy
little villages in Wyoming into boom towns, where crime
grows as fast as the trailer parks."

Marc looked like he was about to reach for Tracy's
hand but then leaned back. "You've seen Brewster. Its
people have roots that go deep. We're just a small
ranching community in the middle of nowhere. Perhaps
the schools aren't number one, perhaps the young
people leave to find work, but zero population growth
doesn't necessarily mean stagnation or the death of a
town. What we have here is unique, and I'd like to keep it
that way as long as possible."

He grinned at her with that smile that always disarmed
her. "There. Now it's your turn on the soapbox."

Tracy knew that everything Marc had said was true.
Brewster would become a wide-open mining town, and
she desperately didn't want that to happen. But she must
play out her part—must continue being Magnum's representative, trying to convince Marc to sell.

"No soapbox needed. Perhaps reading pages eighteen
to twenty-two will help change your mind. Magnum has

set down their terms. Of course, they're negotiable, but I think you'll see that they're very fair to you and the Schells, especially the method of determining tax benefits."

Tracy waited for Marc to read the pages. When he looked up his face had grown pale with a fury she had never seen before. "Is this obscene amount of money supposed to clear my conscience for selling something that doesn't belong to me or the Schells? What a world we live in, where money is used for destruction."

A live coal popped out onto the marble hearth. Marc stood and kicked it back in, then took a poker and struck the logs with a violence that caused a swarm of sparks to shoot up the chimney. He leaned on the mantel, the muscles in his arms tensing as he gripped the marble.

"Tracy, I have one question. Why here? Why not someplace else? Canada is a source that's friendly to America."

"Canada is still a foreign source. You ask why here. Why *not* here? Or are you the type who says, 'Sell me gasoline for my car, but keep the big, smelly oil derricks and refineries in California and Texas. Provide me with coal and all the products made from coal, but let West Virginia have those disfiguring mines. I want lumber for my home, but let the trees in Washington be cut down.' It's easy to sit in an Eden and let the other Edens be exploited for your benefit."

She believed in those ideas, but when the Eden turned out to be Brewster, Idaho, her words tasted bitter in her mouth.

"Now we're getting down to the nitty-gritty. You think I'm selfish trying to keep Idaho only for the Idahoans, don't you?"

Yes, she silently agreed, and realized she didn't blame him. Aloud she said, "What about the Schells? They own that mountain, too."

"Elise will find a way to preserve this place. Kent is rich. She can marry him to keep her precious mansion."

Tracy was shocked. Was that what he thought women did? If they couldn't get what they wanted or needed one way, let them marry for it. Was finding a husband supposed to solve all a woman's problems? What an arrogant, egotistical, self-centered man he was.

Tracy decided to shoot her last gun, even if she hated this argument. Making her voice bland, almost conversational, she said, "Idaho has a long history of mining. I understand that in the early days there were others around here who got their start from mining . . . silver, I believe it was." Her tone became hard and cold. "When you showed me your mountain you didn't mention that Tobias Brewster had help to rape that land. A Mr. Regan and a Mr. Durand all got their shares of the wealth. A Mr. Schell got in on the gravy by marriage. Those people began a dynasty of leading families who have lived very well on that rape-ruin-and-run mining money."

Marc moved close to Tracy and glowered down at her. "Sins of the fathers, Tracy? Should I feel guilty? Or should I continue the practice of making money out of land that doesn't belong to me but to future generations of Americans? If the mountain is sold, Magnum will be the only winner."

"And the people of the United States," she nearly shouted.

Marc was standing over her as if she were a naughty child in school. She set the folders on the table, stood and pulled her shoulders back, readying herself for the bitter words she knew were coming. It was hot in the room now, and the faint odor of wood smoke was making her head ache.

They faced each other, he looking down at her, she with her head bent back to see his angry face.

"I'll answer your question now. Yes, I do think you're

selfish. And as long as we're on the subject, I might as well tell you what else I think." Tracy took a step backward so she could see his face.

"I came here, at your invitation, to see if Magnum and you could work out a simple business proposition. But you took the whole thing as a big joke and acted as if Magnum were a big monster, waiting to devour your mountain. Magnum is a business—out for a profit, yes—but a company that has a reputation for conducting its affairs honorably and fairly."

A wisp of hair had come loose and tickled her forehead. She angrily brushed it aside, hoping that her face showed as little emotion as Marc's. "Since I met you, not once have you taken me seriously as a businesswoman here to negotiate a deal. You've seen me only as a partner for a weekend fling. Well, the weekend is over!"

Tracy didn't have to look at Marc to know that he wore his usual dark scowl. "If you're not willing to sell, say so. Otherwise, I'm wasting my time." She bent down and gathered her folders, shoving them carelessly into the briefcase. Her action was so forceful that she brushed her glasses off the table. They landed on the hearth, then skittered into the fire.

Tracy started to grab for them, but Marc yanked her back. Already the greedy flames were licking at the shiny plastic. "Damn," Tracy said, twisting out of Marc's arms. Grabbing her jacket, she headed for the door, nearly running, thinking only of getting out of this room and away from Marc. She tried to open the heavy sliding doors, but they wouldn't move. She pushed again, then realized that they were locked.

Tracy turned and saw Marc walking toward her, holding the key out in front of him. "Where do you think you're going?"

"First of all, I'm going to tell the Schells the news. Mr. Schell will be overjoyed that the land is saved. Elise can start making her wedding plans. By marrying a wealthy man who she probably doesn't even love she'll solve all her financial problems. You can be best man, I'm sure." Tracy's voice was hard and acid-filled. "Or perhaps *you* could marry her and keep the mountain in the family. That would be even better. Then you'd have won it all. After telling this happy news to Elise, I'm going to pack."

"Pack? Are you leaving?" Marc's eyebrow was raised, giving him an innocent look.

"My job here is finished. I'm driving to Sun Valley this afternoon."

Marc walked over to her. "Sorry, Tracy. That beautiful white stuff out there has closed the highway over the pass. You're not going anywhere for quite a while."

9

~~~~~~~~~~~~~~~

Back in her bedroom, Tracy slammed the door and ran to the window to see Marc walk to his truck. He glanced up and saw her, then removed his cowboy hat with a grand flourish and swept it before him, bending in a courtly bow that would have made a musketeer proud. Even his farewell mocked her, and she longed to throw his stolen fern at him. He regally entered the truck, started the motor and drove off.

Tracy turned from the window, her eyes aching with unshed tears. She placed cold, shaky hands on her cheeks and tried to control her shallow, gasping breaths. She got a damp cloth from the bathroom and washed her face, determined to calm down, to forget how utterly she had failed.

Tracy was stunned to see that it was nearly four o'clock. Where had the time gone? She felt tired and miserable, but the emotional storm she had just experienced had left her too restless to lie down. She forced herself to sit in the large chair by the unlit fireplace. Her eyes closed, and immediately the image of their confrontation formed behind her lids. She could hear their voices filled with bitterness and rancor, and she knew a sadness and pain beyond any she had known before. Tracy didn't regret the things she had told Marc. She had done her best. But now Marc would hate the messenger and that hurt.

Tomorrow she must return to New York—without the Durand land, with nothing but memories. She had allowed Marc to make love to her the night before, and she thought those memories were going to be more than enough. But she had compounded her problem by falling in love, and that had changed everything. Well, what had she expected? An offer of marriage? Did she even want that? She had worked long and hard to get where she was at Magnum. Could she just toss that aside to become a wife, homemaker, mother, pillar of society? Could she completely change her life for marriage? She wouldn't for Eric. Would she for anyone else?

Another dilemma. Solve one and a new one came forth, like the heads of a hydra.

Before Tracy could pursue a solution a buzzing sound startled her. She sat up and looked at her watch. Five-fifteen. The intercom on the wall buzzed again. That couldn't be Marc. Or could it?

Tracy pushed the button and said, "Yes?"

"Miss Cole, it's Pamela from the dining room. A Mr. Allen is on the phone—from New York."

Oh, hell. She was supposed to have called him after she talked to Marc.

"You'll have to come to the sitting room off the main hall. There's no phone on your floor."

"Thanks, Pamela; I'll be right down."

Tracy checked her pale face. Lipstick gone, eyes puffy, her skirt and blouse wrinkled. No time to do anything about it. Feeling misgivings about what she had to tell her boss, she ran downstairs. As soon as she heard Jonathan's gruff voice and told him of Marc's decision, her earlier depression increased.

"What do you mean, he won't sell? Didn't you tell him about the money we're offering and the tax benefits and the environmental protection policy we have?"

"Yes, Jonathan, I told him everything—even offered the absolute maximum terms. He told me he can't sell something that doesn't belong to him."

"What?" he screeched. "The legal department checked. He and the Schells own that area free and clear. Who on earth does he think owns it?"

"Future generations of Americans."

"My God, an idealist." The word was an epithet. Tracy sat down at the desk. Finding an ornately carved jade letter opener lying on top, she held the cold stone against her hot cheek and listened to Jonathan's diatribe about do-gooders and environmentalists, two of his favorite subjects.

After five minutes he paused, and Tracy said, "We can talk about this when I get to New York." The thought of returning gave her an odd sensation in the pit of her stomach.

"Tracy, there might still be a chance. Do you think you could get Durand to Reno?"

"Reno? Why?" What did Jonathan have in mind?

"We have someone out there who could talk to Durand—man to man—and . . ."

Tracy didn't hear the rest. Man to man . . . Had that been a slip, or had Jonathan revealed a well-hidden sexist attitude? Did he think that her abilities were less than a man's, that she had failed with Durand because she was a woman? Jonathan had told her how glad he was to have her with the company, how women should be on boards of directors and not behind ironing boards. Was that just lip service? In his eyes, were she and the other women Magnum employed mere tokens, hired for show?

In Ludlum and here, had she proved him right? No, not right. She *had* the abilities to do the job. In Ludlum there had been forces at work that no one, not even a *man*, could have known about or prevented. In Brewster she faced a man who was obsessed with preserving his land. No one, not even a *man*, could convince him otherwise.

"Tracy! I asked you a question." Jonathan's voice finally penetrated her thoughts.

"What?"

"I said, can you get Durand to Reno tomorrow?"

"I—I don't know. He has a large ranch to run, and with the snow travel is difficult. Besides, I don't think it'll do any good. He won't—"

Ignoring her protests, he said, "Hire a plane if you can't drive. I'll get reservations for both of you for tomorrow night; my secretary will call back and tell you which hotel. When you check in, call me; I'll tell you who to contact. Get Durand to Reno, Tracy. Goodbye, until tomorrow." The buzz of the dial tone filled her ear.

Damn! Now what should she do? When in doubt, eat, she told herself, remembering that she had had no lunch. She'd call Marc, a task she dreaded, after some dinner. Tracy dressed in the blue shirtwaist she had worn the first day. The chrysanthemum petals were still in the pocket. Slipping on her shoes, she smiled, remembering the last time she had worn heels and how Marc had had to carry her. . . . Stop that! she told herself. Concentrate on the negatives of the situation, not the enjoyable times they had had together.

As she walked downstairs, she thought of Elise and the bad news she would have to tell her. Her gaze followed the carpet runner to the library doors, where the old books had been the only witnesses to the unpleasant scene of a few hours earlier. Tracy paused, her hand on the banister, and blinked in surprise at the thought that flashed through her mind. She walked silently down the hall and slid the doors open. The room was already chilly now that the fire had died.

As if she were being drawn by some strange power, her steps led her to the shelves. She picked up a book, the leather on the cover soft and pliable, smelling of saddle soap, and a smile formed on her lips. Elise Schell had another asset besides the now unattainable cobalt in the mountain. Mrs. Quartermain had told her about it the second day she was there: "Brewster's own private collection of books is stored at Mille Fleur House on the second floor." Rich people in Victorian times had filled their libraries with color-coordinated Moroccan-leather-bound books, one more ostentatious display of their wealth.

As if in a treasure hunt where the object was in plain sight, the library, full of first editions, was too obvious for anyone to notice.

Tracy's knowledge of valuable books was limited to what she had witnessed a few months earlier at a major auction house in New York. She had attended their auction of Victorian jewelry, but she had arrived early, in time to see the final bidding on the books. The amount paid for a first-edition Dickens had astonished her. The price for that one book alone could probably pay for the maintenance and preservation of this mansion for years. And there were hundreds of books here, all in excellent condition, the leather well cared for.

When Tracy left in the morning—and somehow she must, with or without Marc—she could at least leave with one positive thing accomplished. Marc's words returned to her: "Kent is rich. She can marry him." Now Elise wouldn't have to marry anyone, Kent or Marc, to find security. Tracy hoped that someday someone would educate Marc about the modern American woman. He certainly needed it.

Tracy enjoyed her dinner much more now that she had one problem solved. She was just leaving the dining room when Marc entered the front door. They paused and stared at each other. Tracy hadn't wanted to see him tonight. The anger and hurt and disappointment were too fresh. She especially didn't want another sparring match with him.

He was smiling warmly, a sure sign of trouble. Tracy watched him warily as he came toward her, his manner the complete opposite of his earlier coldness.

"How lovely you look, Ms. Cole, in your blue dress. What happened to lady executive, type HSF, class 1-A?" Over gray slacks and a white open-neck shirt Marc wore a sheepskin jacket lined with cream-colored curly wool. His dark handsomeness still affected her, and she felt a return of that pleasurable ache deep inside her. But she stifled that response and remembered what she must ask him.

Going right to the point before Marc could find some way to ensnare her physically and emotionally, she said, "Jonathan Allen has asked if you'll fly to Reno with me tomorrow to see another representative. I can hire a plane, or perhaps you'd prefer to fly your own."

Tracy's mood matched her tone of voice. She felt almost numb, almost out of the action, as if she didn't care anymore.

Marc stared at her, disbelief on his face. "What do you mean, take you to Reno? What representative?"

"Jonathan thinks where I've failed, another can succeed . . . a man." Her words were more bitter than she had intended. She had wanted to sound neutral, as if it didn't make any difference. But Jonathan's words had deeply hurt her. She deserved better from someone she had considered a friend.

"Oh, so a rear-guard action has started. They're calling in the reserve troops. A man, you said? Doesn't it hurt your lady-executive soul to have a man called in?"

"Sarcasm isn't necessary, Marc. Even though I told them it wouldn't do any good, they want you to meet with this representative—probably to offer you more money, perhaps even stock options."

Marc laughed and led her to a settee near a front window. Taking one of her hands, he examined it, running his fingers over the smooth back. "Do you think that listening to two representatives is still part of the bet?"

Tracy tried to draw her hand from his. "No, you've paid your debt. I think going to Reno would be a lesson in futility. I'll call Jonathan. . . ."

"Oh, we'll go. I wouldn't miss it. As they say, every man has his price. Perhaps Magnum will find mine." No bitterness tinged his voice. In fact, he seemed to be enjoying himself.

Tracy knew that this trip would prove very interesting, and she dreaded it, yet at the same time she was strangely excited by it.

"Do you suppose I could hire someone to take my rental car back to Sun Valley? Magnum will pay, of course."

"Sam's Garage will do it. I'll make the arrangements." He stood and Tracy followed. "We'll go pack your things. Then you can come to my house, spend the night, and we'll leave early in the morning." He smiled at her, completely at ease, as if no harsh words had ever been spoken.

Tracy hid her anger. He had everything all worked out.

She gave him a night of sexual pleasures and, in return, she got her ride to Reno to see if a male representative could do a better job than she had. You lose, Tracy. Start a new game, throw the dice, go around the board again.

"No, Marc. You can pick me up here in the morning; is 8:30 all right?"

"Why, Tracy, I'm hurt. It sounds as if you're trying to get rid of me."

"I am," she said and walked to the stairs.

Marc's voice echoed in the high-ceilinged room. "OK, 8:30. At least I have Reno to look forward to."

Safe in her room, Tracy wearily undressed. She felt extremely tired. After taking two aspirins, she climbed into bed and turned out the lamp. Trying to relax, she kept thinking of what she would have to face the next day. Who was the representative in Reno? What would she do about Marc once they got there? But before she could find any answers, sleep blotted out everything except her dreams.

10

~~~~~~~~~~

During the trip to Reno Tracy had been uncertain how she should act after the angry words that had passed between them the day before. But Marc wore down her reserved manner, and she found herself relaxing, enjoying the flight over the cultivated fields and ruggedly barren sagebrush country of Idaho and Nevada.

The terrain changed, and Tracy could see the flat alkali desert meld into the gentle rolling hills that surrounded Reno. To the west the towering, snow-covered Sierras acted as a spectacular backdrop to the busy little city. As they approached the airport, Marc pointed out their hotel, which looked regal and aloof, shimmering in the high desert air.

A rental car was ready for them, and they drove the few miles to the hotel. As Marc handed the keys to the bellhop he asked Tracy, "Ever been to Reno?"

"No. I've never even been in a gambling casino before."

Marc laughed, holding the huge glass doors open for her. "What a sophisticated innocent you are."

They walked into the foyer, and Tracy gasped at the

enormity of the room, which was filled with people, hundreds of slot machines and dozens of blackjack, roulette and craps tables. An almost palpable excitement filled the room. Hanging from the red-and-gold ceiling were huge chandeliers made of tiny-faceted crystal and lights that cast a golden glow over the scene.

"The floor is the length of two football fields, Tracy. Impressive, isn't it?" He took her arm and led her to the registration desk that faced the casino floor.

Dragging her attention away from the kaleidoscope of movement and color and sound, Tracy spoke to the smiling desk clerk. "Magnum Mining in New York has reserved rooms for Marc Durand and Tracy Cole."

"Yes, Ms. Cole," she said and efficiently registered them. Handing the bellboy the keys, she smiled and said to Tracy, "Rooms 2180 and 2182. Have a nice stay."

The bellboy opened the door to Room 2180, and all three walked into an entranceway nearly as large as Tracy's apartment's bedroom. To the right was a small powder room. To the left was an L-shaped room with two sofas, numerous chairs, tables and lamps grouped into sitting areas. Against one wall was a dining table that could seat eight. One corner held a curved bar with six tall stools, a sink and a refrigerator.

Tracy was astonished at the size of the room. She followed the bellhop through an archway with folding doors on each side and entered the bedroom. Dominating the room was a king-size bed covered by a brocade canopy that matched the spread. The young man set the suitcases on the luggage racks, accepted Marc's tip, wished them a pleasant stay and left.

Marc, with his arms crossed, was leaning against a door frame. With one eyebrow raised he smiled mischievously.

"Look at this, Tracy. I think I'm going to enjoy our stay in Reno, Nevada."

Tracy walked over to look in, seeing a room lined with blue-and-white tiles, even bigger than her kitchen and bedroom combined. On one side was a glass door with a shower; on the opposite side was a matching door with a bidet. The room even had a phone on the wall.

But the focal point was an eight-foot-square, step-down Roman tub that looked ready for an orgy.

Tracy knew she was blushing; Marc's laughter added to her discomfort.

"You can't blame this on me, Tracy. Allen made the arrangements. Suddenly I like Magnum a little better."

Tracy turned, and with an insouciance she didn't feel, said, "Well, Marc, I wonder what *your* suite is like. Shall we find out?"

The smaller suite next door, decorated in red and gold, had a sitting area, a bathroom and a bedroom with a huge round bed raised on a pedestal.

"I'll take this one," Tracy said. "I'm sure I'll be very comfortable here. After all, you're the one Magnum is trying to impress."

"I accept. Now let's go to the casino and see how much money we can win. How lucky are you?"

"Not very. But you go ahead. I'll find you. I have to make arrangements for us to meet the representative."

"No, I'll wait. Just knock on that door that conveniently connects our rooms." He grinned and sauntered out.

When she called New York both Jonathan and his secretary were out of the office, and the receptionist who took the call didn't know the name of the man in Reno. Tracy told her to have Jon page her at the hotel. Perhaps Magnum's representative was delayed, or perhaps there had been a change of plans and he wasn't coming. Wishful thinking again.

In the elevator going to the main floor Marc said, "When I was walking up to your bedroom to get you this morning I saw Elise coming out of the library with an armload of books. I shouldn't think she'd have time for reading, with all she has to do for Tom and Mrs. Harlow."

"Perhaps she has more time than you think," Tracy said and smiled smugly to herself. The look on Elise's face that morning, when Tracy had told her about the treasure trove in the library, had been marvelous to see.

Tracy had stayed while Elise called a New York auctioneer who specialized in rare books. She had explained about the library, mentioned some of the titles and publication dates and grown more and more pale as she listened to what the man had to say. When she hung up, she had needed to sit down.

"Oh, Tracy," she had said, her hands shaking. "They're sending someone out to look at the books. They'll be here at the end of the week. I just can't believe it." Tears had welled up in her eyes, and she had laughingly wiped them away. "When the woman in charge of the town library came twice a year with high school students to dust and preserve the leather, I always thought it a waste of time. Now . . ." The tears had cascaded down her cheeks, and she had gratefully grabbed the handkerchief that Tracy handed her.

One problem solved, Tracy thought, now, ten more to go.

For the rest of the afternoon Marc and Tracy never stopped, not even taking the time to check the desk to see if Allen had called. They toured the hotel, saw the indoor tennis courts, gym and fifty-lane bowling alley. They visited shops that sold everything from diamond necklaces to kites and dolls, mink coats to souvenir plates with RENO, NEVADA stamped on them in gold. In one shop Marc left her looking at paperweights, explaining that he had something he wanted to buy. He quickly returned and suggested lunch.

As they climbed the wide curved staircase carpeted in red, Tracy realized that being in this hotel was like living in an enclosed city, isolated and self-sufficient, offering every service possible. Yet it had an unreal quality about it. This little town with its restaurants, barber and beauty shops, bank, its wide assortment of entertainment would remain, but the townspeople were transient, constantly moving on to be replaced by new "inhabitants."

"Let me show you the casino now," Marc said after they had finished eating. The feeling of unreality returned when they walked onto the casino floor, which was surprisingly quiet considering the number of slot machines present, many with bells ringing and coins noisily dribbling into metal trays.

Marc bought five rolls of quarters, explaining that they'd start small and work up to bigger things. He ignored Tracy's offer to use her own money, saying, "You can pay me back from your winnings." He explained the operation of the slot machines and jokingly complimented her on her quick mastery of the game. But the greedy, mechanical bandit was also quick at swallowing the quarters.

Next she tried her hand at blackjack, which took her a little longer to understand. It didn't take her long, however, for her to learn that twenty-two didn't win. Marc smiled patiently, and they moved to the craps table, where he showed her what to do. This game was a shade more difficult to understand, but just as quick to take her money.

"Well," Tracy sighed as they walked away from the table, "so much for beginners' luck."

Marc bent down and kissed her neck. "You know the old saying, 'Lucky at love, unlucky at games.' How's your love life?" he whispered in her ear.

"Tracy Cole!" They jumped apart and turned in unison to see a man of medium height standing before them, his sport jacket over one arm.

"Eric Schaeffer!" She gasped the name, then stood in

stunned silence while he kissed her on the lips, a kiss that Tracy had to end herself. Then he stepped back and placed his hands on her arms and said, "Let me look at you."

Tracy glanced over at Marc and, as she had expected, saw a scowl crease his forehead.

"My God, Tracy, you look fantastic." The floor was crowded, and a cocktail waitress bumped into Eric's back with her tray. Glasses tipped, almost toppled, then righted themselves.

"Eric, I would like you to meet—"

Marc grabbed Tracy's arm and interrupted, "Introduce us later. Let's get out of the way."

Tracy and Eric obediently followed Marc up a few stairs to a nearly deserted lounge area that overlooked the gambling arena.

After introducing themselves and ordering drinks from the waitress, they settled back in the soft chairs. As Eric stared longingly at Tracy, Marc frowned and Tracy waited for someone to speak. She still felt a deep sense of shock at seeing Eric. She didn't want this. He was no longer a part of her life, just a finished chapter. Not forgotten, but nothing she wanted to reexperience.

Finally she broke the silence. "I thought you were in South America, Eric."

"I was, but I caught some unpronounceable jungle fever and had to come back. So, until I can return to Guyana, I was sent to check out a possible mine site in Nevada. When Jon Allen told me yesterday you'd be here, well . . ." He picked up his glass and swallowed, trying unsuccessfully to hide his smile.

So Jonathan Allen had known who the representative in Reno was and hadn't told her. When she got back to New York she and Jon were going to have a little talk about honesty and ethics.

Eric turned toward Marc, who was leaning back in his

chair, rolling a silver dollar over the tops of his knuckles. His scowl was gone, replaced by an amused smile.

"Well, Mr. Durand, from what Jon said, you have something Magnum would like to buy. I'm supposed to see if I can offer you a deal you can't refuse."

Tracy winced at Eric's choice of words. Okay, Jonathan Allen, let's just see how a male representative, talking "man to man," will fare when faced with the obdurate, unyielding, uncompromising, stubborn Marc Durand.

The next hour told the story. If Marc had been caustic with Tracy, he was unrelentingly hostile to Eric. The young engineer held his own for a while, but soon began repeating his arguments, rephrasing the sentences so they sounded weaker and weaker.

Tracy said nothing, just divided her attention between the perspiring Eric and the cool Marc, who still flipped the coin over his fingers, back and forth so the light reflected on the shiny face.

Finally Eric smiled and called the waitress to order another round of drinks. Marc and Tracy declined, but Eric had another Scotch and water and said, "I have three reservations for the dinner show. I hope you'll join me."

Marc looked at his watch. "It's four now. Why don't we get ready and meet here for drinks at 6:30? You can explain the stock options then."

Tracy waited for Eric to answer. This was between the two of them, since she was no longer the representative for Magnum. Let Marc deal with the new power.

Eric looked over at Tracy, a pleading look that expressed his love—or was it desire? Before she could say anything Marc stood. "Good," he said, and held out Tracy's chair so she could stand. With an abrupt, "See you at 6:30," they left Eric to finish his drink alone.

With a firm pressure on her arm, Marc silently led her toward the elevator. Tracy had to run to keep up with his long strides. After they had entered his room and the door was shut, Marc turned and said with poorly disguised fury, "What the hell's going on? Eric Schaeffer may have been talking to *me* about cobalt, but he was looking at and thinking only of *you.*" Marc took his jacket off and laid it on the back of the chair.

Using the first defense that came into her head, Tracy said, "Why, Marc Durand, you sound jealous."

"Damn it, Tracy, don't be coy. Who is this joker, and why the long, passionate kiss?"

Tracy gasped at Marc's tone. Again unthinkingly, she asked, "What right have you to ask me about Eric? What about Elise?"

"Elise?" He sounded surprised and confused. "What has Elise got to do with this?" Hands on hips, he glared at her, his dark brows creasing his forehead.

Why had she mentioned Elise? The angry words had come unbidden, a defensive mechanism to combat his accusing words. "I'm sorry I said that. It was unfair and unjustified. I . . ."

"Why did you think there was anything between me and Elise?" His voice was calm, but she could see tension in the way he stood.

Tracy swallowed, ashamed that she had blurted out the accusation. "Blanche told me that everyone in town is speculating whether you or Kent will marry her."

Marc laughed, a reaction that surprised Tracy. "Oh, I see. The town gossip put a bug in your ear. I should have known. Why didn't you ask me?" He paused, waiting for Tracy to respond.

Tracy knew the reason. She had been afraid of the answer, unreasonably and unjustifiably afraid that Marc might be waiting for Elise to recover from Frank's death.

Marc was walking slowly toward her. "You've been thinking I'm in love with Elise." He shook his head, and a lock of hair fell over his forehead. "It was Kent, not I, who

157

wanted Elise all these years. She was in love with Frank, until he finally killed that love with his jealousy." Marc turned and walked to the window, where he stood staring out at the city in the distance. The setting sun turned the sides of the buildings to gold.

Tracy turned so she faced Marc's back. Then he spoke, almost to himself. "Someday Kent will get around to telling her. Right now, all she wants is to save Mille Fleur House, and she blindly believes that selling the mountain is the only solution."

"But . . . well, I know about what happened on the mountain. Elise told me. But why was Frank Harlow . . .?"

Marc turned and walked to the sofa. ". . . jealous of me?" No smile lightened his eyes, and Tracy could read pain in them. "Sit down, Tracy. I'll tell you the whole story."

From the first, Tracy had known that Marc hated talking about himself. She remembered his frowns when she mentioned Vietnam. No mention had ever been made of his wife. Now she was forcing him to explain something that she knew pained him far more.

"Marc, you don't have to . . ." Tracy sat down in a chair opposite him.

"No, Tracy, let's get it all out." He paused, then took a deep breath. "After Elise married Frank I joined the service, not on the rebound, but because it seemed the right thing to do at that moment. When I was wounded I met Abigail, married her and brought her back to Idaho." He stretched his long legs out in front of him, but his relaxed attitude belied the tension on his face. "She hated everything about Idaho, wanted me to return to California. My father was ill by that time, and I wanted to put down roots, to expand the ranch and concentrate on keeping Brewster untouched by the outside world." He paused, and Tracy kept her silence. "Abigail decided that that wasn't what she wanted and left. But she was the kind who always had to have the last word, and as a parting shot she told Frank Harlow that she was leaving because I still loved Elise and that we were having an affair." Marc leaned forward, placing his arms on his knees and clasping his hands together. "That started a cancer that grew; we're still trying to combat the disease."

He sighed and leaned back, running his hands through his hair, further tousling it. Tracy longed to go to him, to rub away the frown that creased his brow, to comfort him. But she couldn't. She had to let Marc take the lead.

In a movement that startled her Marc was on his feet, pulling her up from the chair. The expression on his face was easily readable. Tracy knew just what he was thinking. He could change moods faster than anyone she had ever met. One minute he was lost in the memories of a marriage gone wrong; the next, his eyes full of deviltry, he was planning to take her to bed.

"Marc! I . . . Wait! I still have some questions. Tell me . . ."

Marc stopped her questions with a long kiss. When he finally raised his head Tracy said, "Marc, we're not going to have another big seduction scene. I absolutely refuse to go to bed with you." She twisted away, and Marc let her go.

"OK, Tracy, I agree." His words surprised her, and she stopped backing away, strangely disappointed by his easy capitulation.

Then he grabbed her hand, and Tracy found herself being led through the bedroom into the bathroom.

"Marc!" Tracy tried to squirm away, but only succeeded in losing one of her shoes. Marc slammed the door shut and, holding Tracy by the hand, reached down to turn on the two sets of faucets in the sunken tub. From his pocket he took a bottle and, still holding Tracy, twisted the top off with his teeth and poured the contents under the taps; instantly bubbles spread across the water.

So, Tracy thought, that's what he bought downstairs. He's had this scene planned all along.

"While that fills, we're going to forget Magnum and Eric Schaeffer, and we're going to remove, leisurely and carefully, each other's clothes and—"

"Marc, the only way you'll get me in that tub is to pick me up and throw me in. I will not go willingly."

"Fine. Dressed or undressed?"

Trying again to escape his arms, she slipped and would have fallen if Marc hadn't caught her.

"If you fall, the question will be conscious or unconscious."

The room was filling with steam, and Tracy's blouse and wraparound skirt were clinging to her. Marc, too, looked hot, but it didn't seem to deter him from concentrating on Tracy's clothes.

"Tracy, why does everything you own have these damn buttons? Haven't you heard of zippers?"

Tracy twisted away from his insistent fingers. A button popped off, flew across the room and landed in the fast-filling bathtub.

"You're making this very difficult."

"Marc, I mean it. I want you to stop." Tracy's words were said less vehemently than she had intended. Why couldn't she make her voice sound more convincing? Or could it be that she wanted a renewal of that passion that had overcome her, giving her such pleasure? Marc desired her as a woman, and she desired him. But was it worth the future pain of knowing that that was all she meant to him? "Marc, I do *not* want this."

"You've said that before." Marc unknotted her belt.

The skirt almost fell to the floor, but he grabbed it and set it on the counter.

With deceptive calm Tracy said, "If you do this, I'll . . . I'll . . ."

Marc stopped taking off his own shoes and looked up at her. "What will you do, Tracy? Remember, you're not the hysterical type."

Marc tried to straighten up, but one stockinged foot slipped and he fell, pulling Tracy down on top of him.

"Oh, damn, that hurt," he said and disentangled his arms from Tracy's so he could rub his elbow. Despite the pain in Marc's eyes, she began to laugh at the whole ludicrous scene. Through the scent-filled steam she could see a waterfall of bubbles and water begin to pour over the edge of the tub. Leaving Marc holding his injured elbow, she crawled over to turn off the water. Disregarding her shirt, she reached into the tub, trying to find the handle to open the drain. At last the water level began to go down. Tracy tried to shake the water off her arm and didn't see Marc move over to her until he reached in and closed the drain. When they looked at each other, covered with bubbles, sitting on the tile floor in two inches of water, their laughter erupted simultaneously.

Tracy took a handful of foam and dabbed it on Marc's chin so that it resembled whiskers. "Now I know what you'll look like when you're old." The minute the words were out she realized how they must sound.

"Oh? So you think you'll be around when I'm a white-haired dirty old man?"

"Instead of a black-haired lecherous young man?" Tracy smiled, then suddenly sobered and started to get up. But with a movement so fast that it was just a blur to her eyes, Marc grabbed her arm and forcibly drew her toward him. On the slick floor she easily slid across and tumbled into his arms. Her soaked shirt clung to her skin, revealing her lacy bra, and she held her breath as Marc's admiring gaze traveled over her, missing nothing. His face became serious, the mocking, teasing look gone. Seeing desire clearly in his eyes, Tracy felt the now familiar, rapid rhythm of her heart drumming in her ears.

Marc reached out and touched her breast tenderly, as if afraid of her reaction. "Tracy, I wish I had the words to tell you how beautiful I think you are."

A feeling of enchantment came over Tracy. She didn't want to fight him anymore. Eric's assignment as representative had relieved her of her responsibilities. She was free. She hoped that what she was about to do was right.

Reaching over, she began to unbutton Marc's shirt. "Seems silly to waste all this water. . . ."

The tub proved to be just a little too small for swimming, but plenty large enough for anything else. Each time Marc tried to grab Tracy to kiss her she teasingly slipped away, laughing at his frustration. Marc slid over to sit on a submerged ledge and tried to wipe the suds off to see his arm. "I think I've cracked my elbow. It's swelling and hurts like hell."

Without thinking Tracy crawled over to see and Marc caught her, enfolding her against his body. An excited anticipation coursed through her. Breathlessly she said, "Your injured arm hasn't affected you too adversely."

Marc said nothing, just smiled and, with little puffs of air, blew the iridescent bubbles off one of her breasts. He rubbed the other with his fingers. The slippery sensuousness of the act sent an intense, throbbing ache through Tracy. Marc took one dark-red bud in his mouth and alternated between sucking at it and running his tongue rapidly over it, matching the pulsating beat deep within her.

"Oh, Marc," she gasped, the words barely passing her constricted throat. Unable to stand it any longer, she lifted his head and found his lips, kissing him in a way that left no doubt about what she was experiencing. As their tongues sought each other Marc continued to rub her body, the sudsy water increasing the sensuality. They leaned against the slanted back of the tub and when they moved, the water swirled around them, the bubbles forming a whirlpool of multicolored orbs.

Marc cradled Tracy's neck in his arm and drew her close. He trailed his fingertips over her body, gliding them across her stomach, then moving them up to her smooth, round breasts. His featherlike touch caused Tracy to murmur her pleasure. Marc's own unintelligible purr revealed that he, too, was affected. As his hand grew increasingly bold his mouth sought hers with a hunger that wouldn't be denied. When his lips moved to the hollow at the base of her neck Tracy was again aware of his hand as it waltzed around her body. With each touch, as if attached to a string, her muscles flexed, and Tracy writhed and arched her response. In her mind she screamed to have him stop, to end this before she lost all control.

Marc did stop. Still kissing her until they were both breathless, he placed her hand on his chest. When Tracy hesitated Marc lifted his head and said, "Yes, Tracy, your touching me and learning what a man feels like is part of the experience." He smiled at her, a look that bespoke his desire and passion, precursors of love.

Tracy slipped her hand out of Marc's, never taking her eyes from his half-closed, emotion-filled ones. Tentatively at first, then with a boldness that surprised both of them, she explored Marc's body, and his resultant moan told her what this action did to him.

"My God, Tracy, let's get out of here. Please . . . I must . . ."

He grabbed a large towel and helped a weak Tracy to

stand as he wrapped it around her: then they stepped out of the tub. With what seemed like maddening slowness Marc dried her, each stroke sending shivers of anticipation through her. In the steamy mirror Tracy saw their naked bodies in a surrealistic, erotic pose that she would remember for the rest of her life.

Lifting her in his arms, he carried her to the bed and with one hand pulled back the spread and gently laid her down. The room was cool after the hot bath, and the sheets felt slightly rough to her overly sensitized skin. Marc looked down, his gaze roaming over her as if reveling in the sight of her, while Tracy's gaze traveled over his own beautiful body.

Tracy smiled and murmured, "Hurry, Marc, I don't think I can . . ."

He lay down beside her and immediately pulled her warm body against him. Then, with expertise and patience, with an insistence that wouldn't be denied, Marc again accompanied Tracy on her journey. Tracy forgot her surroundings, was aware only of what his mouth was doing, how his tongue found the secret places that his hands had discovered earlier, sending sensations through Tracy so intense that she shouted his name, her nails leaving long, red streaks down his back.

Then Marc changed tactics, letting the throbbing of her body begin to slow down, allowing her to catch her breath, her heart to stop racing. When she was more in control he started again by kissing her fingertips, her palms, her arms. He paused to murmur his delight at her beauty, then continued trailing kisses to her mouth, her loosened hair, her breasts, moving to areas that brought her unimagined pleasure. Each time he stopped, Tracy would feel her passion increase, and she would moan and arch her hips, lost in the hedonistic sensuality that washed over her.

Tracy's movements revealed how near she was to losing control. Soon, very soon, she wouldn't be able to stop her body's responses, and she would slip over the edge into a world of private delights.

Marc slowed his actions and said, "Not yet, Tracy. Wait for me."

Tracy lay panting, her hands clutching the sheet on each side of her. With little, light kisses, Marc's mouth slowly moved up her flat stomach to her breasts, to her waiting lips and over to her ear. He whispered, "Now it's your turn." He lifted his head and looked down at her.

Tracy smiled at him. Even though he sounded calm, his eyes were dark with desire. Tiny beads of sweat dotted his forehead and she reached up to wipe them away. He was quivering, too, his breath rapid and shallow. At his neck an artery imitated the fast beat of his heart.

This time Tracy knew what she was doing. With sureness and confidence she began to make love to Marc, instinctively refining the techniques he had shown her. Tracy had learned a few things while they had been in the water. Wanting to give him sensations as intense as she had just experienced, she let her hand explore Marc, working a magic that soon sent him near his own brink. She stopped, letting his gasping breath return to normal.

With fingers, mouth, teeth and tongue, Tracy again teasingly tantalized Marc, touching him, kissing him in places she knew would give him satisfaction. Using the Braille method to learn what his body felt like, and holding nothing back, Tracy increased her own enjoyment a thousandfold.

With each stroke of her hand she marveled at the symmetry of his perfect body. Pressing her hands and lips to the smooth, tanned skin that covered his hard muscles, Tracy gloried in the touch, the scent, the taste of Marc Durand.

"My God, Tracy," Marc gasped. "You're an incredibly fast learner." Each word was spoken slowly, as if his reactions to Tracy were so strong that expressing them was difficult.

"I had a good teacher."

By unspoken agreement, both slowed their actions, each wanting to prolong the sweet torment. Tracy placed little kisses around his mouth. Marc's hands roamed up and down her back, while he murmured words of admiration for her body. Using light strokes, Tracy began running her fingertips over Marc's face, over his high cheekbones and the slight bump in his nose. She must ask him about that sometime. But not now . . .

She moved down to his chest, down his abdomen and onto his hip. There she found a faint scar that continued on around until she could no longer trace it. Was this why he had been in the military hospital? Curiosity forced her to open her mouth to ask him what it was, but suddenly she was on her back with Marc again the aggressor, effectively stopping her question. Without a word, he renewed his arousal of her until she moaned and twisted under him. Her whispered repetition of his name communicated to Marc her need to end her agony by the joining of their bodies. When he entered her she was filled with a sense of rightness that changed an age-old ritual into something almost holy. She felt fragile, as if she could shatter into a million pieces. She held her breath, afraid to break the moment. Marc stopped and looked down at her, instinctively seeming to know that she was experiencing something that transcended the physical act of love. Slowly, carefully, she released her pent-up breath and smiled at Marc.

"Tracy, Tracy. Are you all right? Did I . . .?" He never finished his sentence. With one shaking hand she pulled his head down to her welcoming mouth and they both became lost in their world of sensations and desire and passions, each sharing and accepting, each demanding and yielding.

After an immeasurable amount of time reality returned. At last they could breathe normally, their racing hearts slowing. They smiled at each other. Tracy's hair was tangled, and Marc unsuccessfully tried to smooth it.

With the return of normalcy Tracy asked herself if she cared that Marc had again proved that she was powerless to resist him. No. She knew each time Marc used that power he came closer to discovering that he not only wanted her but that he loved her. And Marc's fierce lovemaking had told her one thing: She was more to him that just someone to have sex with.

"Marc, you told me our experience Sunday night was unbelievably rare and wonderful. Well, what we just had far surpassed it." She whispered the words, her voice tremulous. She had to pause to gain control over her emotions.

To hide the tears she couldn't hold back she placed her head under Marc's chin, breathing deeply of his scent. Running her tongue along the strong cords of his neck she tasted her own tears and the saltiness of Marc's skin. She found his hand and slipped her fingers between his.

"Thank you, Tracy," he murmured, his lips pressed to her hair.

Would she ever understand this man? Perhaps that was what made him so delightful. He could shock her, irritate her, surprise her, keep her off guard. But she couldn't deny that the perfect, satisfying mating of their two bodies made her feel incredibly, wonderfully, unalterably alive.

She didn't raise her head, just lay next to him, glorying in the feelings of calm euphoria and happiness that were such a contrast to their earlier tempest. She felt as if she were in a . . . safe harbor? She silently laughed. If Marc were a safe harbor, she would hate to see the fury of the ocean.

11

~~~~~~~~~~~~~

Marc sighed, a sound that communicated his own satiation. He reached over and drew Tracy on top of him so she lay along his full length. As if he never wanted to stop, he ran his hands up her thighs, over her rounded buttocks, finally arriving at her breasts. Looking deeply into her eyes, he said, "Tracy, I want you to know that I . . ." A sound came and made Marc groan. "Damn." The phone rang again. Tracy reached for it, but Marc held her back. "Ignore it," he demanded harshly. Another ring.

"Marc, that's probably Eric wondering where we are. I have to answer it." She stretched out to reach for the receiver. "Hello?"

Marc took her free hand in his and led it to his body, letting her know that he was again ready to make love to her. She gasped and tried to remove her hand, but he held on tightly, moving his other hand to touch her in places that he knew would reignite her passion. As they silently struggled Tracy stammered out, "What? Oh, nothing's wrong." She put her hand over the receiver and mouthed the words, "Marc, stop that."

Into the receiver she said, "No, I don't know where Marc is. Maybe gambling. I didn't feel well this morning on the plane so I—I took a little nap."

Marc kissed the damp hair at the back of her neck and whispered, "Beautiful liar."

To escape the incredible sensations that were again flowing through her body Tracy moved as far away from Marc as she could and tried to concentrate.

"Eric, I'll be down soon. Wait for me in the lounge. Marc will find us, I'm sure." She paused, listened and said, "Yes, Eric, I was glad to see you again, too. I have to go. See you soon."

She hung up and said, "I'm going to get dressed . . . Marc! Stop . . ." Their kiss lasted a long time, body pressed to body.

Finally Marc lifted his head and said, "Tracy, even though it'll be difficult, we'll get dressed and go down to hear Eric offer me a deal I can't refuse. But in return"— Marc ran his hand down Tracy's back—"you have to promise to spend the night with me. I want to awaken in the morning to find you beside me."

"Marc, I can't promise that." Tracy felt that she had to make Marc declare his love for her then, or else he never would.

"Why?" His voice was calm, belying the tension she felt in his body.

"Because tonight I . . . I'm going back to New York, to my job, if I still have one. If not . . ." She shrugged.

Now, Marc, say it now. Say you want Tracy Cole, formerly of New York, to return with you to Brewster, Idaho, where you two, working together, can help that slumbering community find a new life without any negative outside influences. Say it now. . . .

"What do you mean, return to New York? Why the sudden turn-off, especially after what we just experi-

170

enced? Did that call from Eric Schaeffer have anything to do with this? What is he to you, anyway?"

Tracy slipped from Marc's arms, got quickly out of bed and walked on shaky legs toward her suitcases, which were still in his room. She said nothing, just found a wool dress, underwear and shoes and sat on the bed to dress. Trying not to think that Marc was watching her every move, she said, "Eight months ago I broke our engagement."

"Engagement!" Marc got up, walked over and glowered down at her. "Why didn't you marry him?"

"Marc, stop standing over me as if I were a naughty child."

He stepped closer and said, "Tracy, I want an answer."

She took a deep breath and replied, "He wanted me to quit my job and follow him wherever Magnum sent him." Bra and pantyhose on, she reached for her slip.

"And you refused?"

"I worked just as hard and as long as he did for a career. If he had wanted to marry me, he could have stayed in New York—not asked *me* to quit." With her dress on, she struggled to close the back.

"*Now* you wear something with a zipper," he muttered and coldly zipped it up, not touching her. More loudly he said, "A mining engineer in New York City?" He wrapped the wet towel around his waist.

Tracy's face remained somber. "Irreconcilable differences. We just found them out before marriage, not after." She sounded cool and detached, as if she were talking about someone else, not about something that had hurt for so long. . . .

"Do Magnum and a career mean that much to you?" He spoke in a low tone, saying the words slowly, almost as if he feared hearing her answer.

"Marc, I really don't want to talk about this. What

difference does it make? It's over and we both know it."

She was talking about her and Marc, not about Eric. Her throat ached; tears would have fallen if she hadn't willed them away. Without Marc's love the Idaho affair had ended.

"You really do believe in the 'what's good for the goose' bit, don't you?"

"Damn right, I do." She turned to look at him. "You had better get ready."

Tracy slipped on her high heels and, except for make-up, was ready. Taking her cosmetic case, she went to the dresser and combed her still damp hair, pinning it in a coil on top of her head. She quickly put on some lipstick and was finished. Marc had opened his own suitcase and was dressing, strangely silent.

Without being obvious Tracy put her wet blouse and skirt in a plastic bag and packed them. She closed the cases and set them with her other luggage.

"I'm ready, Marc," she called to him. "I'll go down and pacify Eric until you come."

Marc said nothing, and she couldn't see his face. She picked up her handbag and key, leaving him to his own thoughts.

On the main floor she stopped by the front desk, signed the charge-card slip to pay for the rooms, explaining that Suite 2182 would not be needed and that Mr. Durand could use the other room for as long as he wanted.

She found the travel desk and asked about flights to New York. There was one at ten o'clock, which would be perfect.

Eric was looking worriedly at his watch when she sat down, and his face broke into a smile of welcome.

"Oh, Tracy, I'm so glad to see you." His voice dropped so only she could hear. "After the show, let's get rid of

Durand and, well . . ." Under his tan he blushed and Tracy knew what he had in mind.

"Eric, please don't think about renewing our relationship. I still feel the way I did before."

"But, Tracy, I still want you." He took her hand, looking ardently into her eyes. He hadn't said love, Tracy noticed. Wanting meant only one thing.

"Am I interrupting anything?" Marc asked with sweetness dripping from his voice. He pulled out a chair to sit near Tracy. Under the table their legs touched; Tracy moved away and Marc grinned at her. His earlier anger seemed to have disappeared. He was certainly a changeable man.

With something akin to hatred in his eyes Eric said, "How was the gambling?"

Marc looked directly at Tracy and said, "Oh, I won. I nearly always win, don't I, Tracy?" He turned to Eric and asked, "How's the jungle fever?"

Before Eric could respond the cocktail waitress came to their table. Eric looked at his watch and said, "We have time for just one drink before we have to go in for dinner." He handed Marc some papers and said, "Here's the new offer Magnum is making for your land, Marc."

While Marc read the handwritten pages Eric and Tracy talked of people they both knew, about the new bauxite find in Australia, about Magnum's new president. Finally Eric looked at his watch and said, "We'd better go to our seats."

Tracy heard Marc sigh and suspected that he really didn't want to see the dinner show or even be in the same town with Eric Schaeffer. As an instinctive reaction to Marc's dislike of Eric, she allowed Eric to take her arm and escort her across the casino to the dining room entrance, with Marc trailing behind them.

The room looked like a theater, with a stage and

curtain, but instead of seats it had tiers lined with tables and chairs where two thousand dinners could be served. After they were seated and had ordered Eric turned to Marc and said, "How do you like Magnum's new deal?"

"Mr. Schaeffer," Marc said, and Tracy knew what was coming, "the amount of money in the first offer was outrageous. This is even worse."

"But, Marc, uh, Mr. Durand, this is extremely generous. Having stock options in a company with the growth potential of Magnum is worth much more . . ."

Marc's quiet voice interrupted. "Oh, you misunderstand me. Both deals are ostentatiously generous. What I'm saying is that under no circumstances, regardless of how much money is offered, will I sell my land. Magnum and the United States government will have to find cobalt somewhere else, at least as long as I have a say in the matter. Do I make myself clear?"

It was perfectly clear to Tracy. Now she knew for certain. Never before had Marc come out and bluntly said that he would not sell. This was what she had known he would say, but until he had, she could do nothing. Now she could.

"Eric, Marc, please excuse me. I'm going to the ladies' room."

Before they could move she had grabbed her handbag and rushed from the crowded room. She practically ran through the casino, seeing the colored lights and people only as a blur. She found the note paper she had taken from the room, wrote short notes of explanation to both Eric and Marc, and asked a waiter to deliver them in fifteen minutes. Finding a bellhop, she handed him the key and explained what luggage to bring down. The airport limousine waited for her while she tipped the attendant, then Tracy was driven away from the hotel and all its memories. She saw the lights of Reno through the refracted vision of unshed tears.

12

The Tracy Cole who walked into the small New York apartment early Wednesday morning was not the same one who had left the previous Thursday. While she unpacked she realized that in those few days she had grown a little older and a lot wiser, and with this new maturity came questions. What was she going to do about her future with Magnum? What about Marc Durand?

Knowing she was too tense to sleep, she took a long bath that brought back memories so painful that the tears she had fought all night finally came. The emotional release solved nothing, so she went to bed, but when she awoke after two hours' sleep she still felt exhausted and irritable.

The minute she arrived at her office later that morning she knew she should have delayed seeing Jonathan Allen.

"Tracy, you look terrible." Without waiting for a reply he continued, "What the hell happened in Reno? Eric just called and said the whole deal was off and that you would explain."

On the plane the night before Tracy had written a report giving the sequence of events, leaving out the personal details. She handed the papers to Jonathan and sat back to stare out the window while she waited for him to read them.

When he looked up anger had made his face turn red. "Well, you really blew it."

The words hit Tracy like a slap, and she experienced a fury she had never felt before. "Oh, no, you don't. You can't assume that I blew it. Didn't Eric tell you how adamant, unyielding and stubborn Marc Durand was? Nothing would have made any difference, because he wasn't about to sell that land to anyone."

"What do you mean? Why did he send for a representative then?" His voice was as cold as his expression.

"Marc played poker with Elise Schell, and the stakes were that he'd at least listen to a representative. He was only paying off a gambling debt. He never had any intention of selling."

The silence lasted a long time while Jonathan absorbed what Tracy had just revealed. While she waited she planned what to say next, wanting to put Jonathan on the defensive. Finally she said, "Now I want an explanation of why you sent someone to take over my assignment and why you didn't tell me it was Eric Schaeffer."

Another long silence ensued while they stared at each other. Jonathan lit a cigarette. "Eric was in the area; he was the logical choice. I didn't tell you because I didn't want to upset you. I thought I'd get a chance to talk to you before you met Eric." He paused, then said, "You think my having Eric talk to Marc was an insult to your abilities?"

"To put it bluntly, yes, I do."

"Well, I'm not going to apologize. Magnum desperately needs that land. We've already spent thousands on the project. I'd have sent in the Marines if I thought it would have done any good. Eric said Durand just laughed when he told him about the stock options."

"That's right. There are some people who can't be bought, Jon, but I don't suppose you've met any in your long career."

"Not many. But I have seen people like those two in Ludlum, Farnsworth and Bishop, who got greedy and sold out to Owens Mining. Perhaps if we'd had a man there, that wouldn't have happened."

Tracy stood and leaned on Jonathan's desk. "OK, let's say it all. Let's tell the story of Magnum and its new liberal president who allowed women into the company's executive training program. But some of the employees who were here when it was a male sanctum sanctorum haven't quite accepted the new plan. And you're one of them, aren't you?" Without waiting for an answer, she sat down, her knees suddenly shaky. "Your little speech about how women should be on boards of directors was just to sound good, trying to comply with the new president's wishes. Isn't that right, Jon?"

Jonathan shrugged and said, "You're doing the talking." He stubbed out his cigarette and lit another.

"I have one more thing to say. You had better get used to having women in the business world, because we're here to stay."

"And you, Tracy? Are you here to stay?"

In that moment Tracy resolved one of the problems that had haunted her since seeing Brewster and Marc's mountain. She remembered how affected she had been by the area and how she had longed to agree with Marc's powerful arguments. His words had reinforced her own growing doubts, but it wasn't until this moment that she had known what she wanted. She wanted to preserve places like that, not be part of a company that tore open the land and consumed the natural resources, making money for investors who cared nothing for wilderness areas. Perhaps mining activities were necessary, but she didn't have to be part of them.

"No, Jon, I'm not staying. I'm resigning, and when you inform our esteemed president, tell him the reasons. Tell him that Mr. J. B. Allen is sexist and that Miss Tracy Cole found out before it was too late." She took a deep breath and added. "But don't think I'm quitting because of you. A hundred men with your attitude couldn't make me leave if I still believed in what I was doing. But Magnum and I no longer have anything in common."

"So, Eric was right. He said you and Durand had become lovers. You must have caught a bad case of idealism."

Tracy gasped. Eric must have suspected what was happening when he called her room, and he must have spread the word to Jonathan. Thank you, Eric, she whispered silently. Pulling her shoulders back in an act of defiance, she stood tall and said, "Idealism is something you'll never have to worry about. You're immune."

She turned and walked out the door, knowing that she had just fallen off the corporate ladder for good and all. Where she landed she didn't really care, as long as it wasn't anywhere near a mine, Magnum or Jonathan Allen.

Going directly to a supply room she found a box, cleaned out her desk, made arrangements to have her things delivered to her apartment, said her goodbyes and left.

Three years to climb, one hour to fall.

Still feeling numb from the shock, Tracy made arrangements to leave a New York that no longer held any excitement for her. Perhaps in the Bahamas she could forget the past week. But instead of beaches, palm trees and ocean, she saw twisting canyons, aspen and pine trees and snow-covered mountains. Every man she met had about as much personality and charm as a life-size

178

cardboard cutout. Marc filled her daytime thoughts and her nighttime dreams. She forced herself to stay in the Caribbean for two weeks. When she returned to her empty apartment, her face was tanned to a golden tone, but her eyes still had a lost, haunted look.

Without unpacking, she got her mail from her neighbor. Nothing from Marc Durand. Disappointed, she blinked back the tears. But there were four letters and a telegram, all from a Symbios Foundation in Boulder, Colorado. She opened the telegram. It was a request that she contact them as soon as possible and was signed by Ms. Sylvia Gold. Confused, Tracy put the letters in order according to date. The first one had a color brochure that told about Symbios, a private foundation that was dedicated to protecting the environment. All the letters said that they were very interested in having her talk to their recruiter at her convenience. Tracy smiled. It hadn't taken an executive headhunting service long to find out she had left Magnum.

During the next week two more letters and another telegram came, all signed by Sylvia Gold. Tracy's interest was piqued by their persistence. Knowing that she had to shake off her lethargy by doing something besides stare into space thinking of Marc, she called a friend at Magnum's research department and had her check on the Symbios Foundation. Within an hour she had learned that it was a small, three-year-old, nonprofit, well-financed organization that already had an excellent reputation among historians and environmentalists in the West. Its latest accomplishment had been working with the Colorado Historical Society to save an old locomotive from being junked.

Tracy thanked her friend and found the dictionary to check the unusual name of the foundation. Symbios was from a Greek word meaning "one living together with another, a partner, an association where neither is harmed and one or both benefit." Tracy thought it was an apt name for a company dedicated to making the earth one place for all. She immediately telegraphed that she'd meet with their representative at noon, any day of the following week, and named a restaurant. A telegram arrived, setting the date and time, and changing the locale to a midtown hotel.

Tracy sent a succinct confirmation and waited anxiously for the time to pass. Finally the day arrived. She dressed carefully in a modified version of her lady executive uniform and wondered what Marc would have said about the feminine touches she added. The pain of remembering Marc had not lessened. She sighed and went outside into the snow to look for a taxi.

The hotel, with its quiet elegance, reminded Tracy of Mille Fleur House. She laughed at herself. Almost everything brought back memories of Idaho.

On the dot of noon she knocked on the door of the Symbios suite. No one came. She checked the number and had just raised her hand to knock again when the door swung open to reveal a tall man. The light was behind him and at first Tracy couldn't see who it was.

"Ms. Cole?" As soon as she heard the voice she knew.

"Marc Durand," she whispered.

Tracy couldn't force her legs to move. Her mind refused to accept the shock of seeing this man here. Where was the representative from Symbios? "What's going on?"

"Tracy, wipe the stunned look off your face and let me shut the door." He took her arm and led her into a sitting room.

Tracy sat on the first chair she came to, her legs suddenly weak. Taking a shallow breath, she said, "Marc, what kind of game are you playing now?"

"Why, Ms. Cole, how can you ask that? I assure you

that I have no ulterior motive for asking you here today. I'm here to interview you for a job."

"You always have a reason for everything you do. It doesn't take much intelligence to see your plan. Well, not this time." She stood and headed for the door, but Marc stopped her before she had gone three steps. His touch sent a shock through her body, and her heart began to race, sending a message to her brain, reminding her of what this man could do to her. Why did she always respond like this? What chemistry existed between them so that, when she was near him, all she could think about was letting his body enfold hers in a never-ending embrace?

But this time, she vowed, the chemistry wouldn't work. Before, Marc had had everything his way. Now *she* would call the shots. She stepped back, trying to escape his disturbing touch. But Marc easily held her. An expressive smile curved his mouth, and Tracy knew that he was enjoying her obvious confusion.

"Tracy, calm down and listen to me. Why are you acting like this?"

"Because you tricked me. You sent those letters and telegrams from Symbios with not one word about who the recruiter was. And what have you got to do with Symbios anyway? How are you involved?" All the unhappiness and heartache she had felt for the previous five weeks boiled to the surface, and she yanked her arm away. "My leaving Reno must have been quite a blow to your male pride for you to make these elaborate plans . . . letters and telegrams and fancy hotel suites."

In three long strides Marc was at the desk, telephone in hand, punching the buttons in rapid succssion. He turned and looked at Tracy, who had not moved. Their gazes locked; they stood suspended in a moment of anticipation.

"Hello, Kent? This is Marc. Would you tell Tracy about Symbios?" He paused, listened, then said, "Kent, don't be cute. Just tell her the truth." Marc held the phone out to Tracy. His expression told her that she had better listen to what Kent had to say.

"Hello? Yes, Kent, I'm fine." Tracy silently listened to Kent's deep rumbling voice. With each passing moment her astonishment increased.

"Before Marc's father died, he set up a trust fund to be used for protecting the environment and endangered species and for preserving important historical sites. With that money, Marc organized the foundation. I'm on the board of directors, as are a number of other men and women in Idaho and Colorado."

"But why wasn't I told?"

"Marc asked me not to. I don't know why."

Tracy sat on the edge of the desk and looked around for Marc. He was near the window, his arms on either side of the frame, leaning forward, staring out at the snow.

Tracy turned her back and said, "It must be some organization that will ignore the town of Patience. . . ."

Kent gave a low laugh. "It's like Elise and the books. Too obvious for anyone to see. Marc has proposed to the board that this area be next on the agenda." She could hear him puff on his pipe. "Tracy, Symbios is legitimate. Marc is actively searching for more people to join the organization."

Tracy lowered her voice and asked, "Kent, do you have any more of your hometown homilies? Any words of advice?"

She could hear the laughter in Kent's voice as he said, "Nope. You're on your own, Tracy."

"Thanks a lot." She wondered if she should ask her next question. "How's Elise?"

A long pause increased her doubt. Then she heard a match strike and visualized Kent relighting his pipe. "She wouldn't have me when she was poor. Now, well, I'm going to marry a rich widow."

A smile erased Tracy's frown. "Oh, I'm so happy for you both. Please give her my congratulations."

"Thanks, I will. We'll send you an invitation. Good luck, you'll—"

"I know, I'll need it. Goodbye, Kent." She slowly lowered the receiver and turned toward Marc. He continued to stare out the window, saying nothing. In the silence the cacophony of the city filtered up from the street thirteen floors below.

Tracy had to make a decision. Marc hadn't turned around. He was leaving it up to her. She could walk out now or stay and listen to the recruiter from the Symbios Foundation. She asked herself if she still wanted to consider employment with a company diametrically opposed to Magnum. Yes, came the answer. But would it make any difference if Marc were the employer? That depended on what Marc was offering. Well, she'd have to find out.

"OK, Marc, I understand about the Symbios Foundation. Why didn't you tell me about it before?"

Marc turned and moved toward her, his expression still unfathomable. "You weren't ready to listen. But now you're no longer employed by Magnum."

He waited for her to reply, but she remained silent, watching him come closer. "I can imagine what kind of report Eric Schaeffer made. After we received your little farewell letters he had a great deal to tell me about the lovely Ms. Tracy Amanda Cole."

"Marc, we aren't here to discuss Eric or my leaving Magnum. What about Symbios?" Tracy moved back until she could go no further. She felt her breath quicken at his nearness. The chemistry still worked. In fact, it seemed more powerful now, its potency increasing every moment.

"But your leaving Magnum is what we have to discuss." Marc inched forward until he was towering over her, making Tracy again aware of his height and strength and complete maleness. She tried unsuccessfully to take a deep breath, her eyes revealing her reaction to his overpowering presence.

"Marc, d-don't . . ." She stopped speaking; her brain seemed to have ceased sending messages to her tongue. She waited for Marc's next move.

"Tracy, come to me," Marc whispered, and the words were the most beautiful sounds she had ever heard. He held his hand out. With no conscious thought on her part, her own lifted and found his. At the touch a shock rocketed through Tracy that made her knees buckle, and if Marc hadn't caught her she would have fallen. When their lips met all the sensations she had experienced when he had made love to her returned. She felt a renewal of the desires and passions that had been denied so long.

But when Marc lifted her in his arms Tracy found the strength to say, "Marc, unless you have something more to offer me than one exciting night, I suggest you put me down. Regardless of what you may think, promiscuity is not my game. Playtime ended in Reno."

"I know, Tracy. I want to offer you a job—one with fringe benefits."

"Marc, before any discussion of fringe benefits, you'd better tell me what's involved in this job offer. We talk or else I leave right now."

Her face showed her seriousness. Marc's expression changed, as if he realized that Tracy meant what she said. After walking over to the sofa he sat down, with her on his lap.

"Not this way, Marc. You in one chair, me in another. When we're too close we seem to forget the purpose of our discussion." Tracy was pleased with her firm tone of voice.

Marc sighed his resignation, and Tracy slipped off his lap and walked toward a chair opposite the sofa. "I want some honest answers from you. Why this subterfuge? Why didn't you tell me about Symbios?"

"You drive a hard bargain."

"I had a good teacher."

Marc smiled and leaned back in his chair, reminding Tracy of their confrontation in the library of Mille Fleur House. "I resorted to subterfuge, as you call it, because I wanted you to change your mind on your own about Magnum. By quitting and coming here today, you proved what your sentiments now are." He crossed his long legs, and Tracy noticed for the first time that he was dressed like a successful executive, complete with exquisitely tailored suit, subdued tie and white shirt, a sharp contrast to the casual clothes he had worn on the ranch. Had this Symbios recruiter interviewed anyone else today, or was this all for the ex-Magnum employee?

"You seemed so intent on spreading Magnum's line that I knew nothing I said would do any good. But, since you're obviously adamant about having a career, I thought it would be better to have you in a company I run so there wouldn't be any conflict of interest. We don't want to find we have any irreconcilable differences that could lead to divorce."

The word was dropped so casually that Tracy didn't catch it at first. Marc's expression hadn't changed; he just sat watching her as he would an opponent in a poker game.

"Divorce?" Tracy spoke in a voice barely audible. "What does that mean?"

Marc started to stand, but Tracy's next words stopped

him. "Don't you move, Marc Durand. You sit right there until you tell me what you mean."

He laughed, a deep rumbling sound that Tracy had heard in her mind a hundred times in the past few weeks.

In one swift movement Marc was standing before Tracy, taking her cold hands in his, tugging her to her feet. His eyes showed anxiety and . . . pain.

"Tracy, these past weeks have been hell, not knowing if I had let you get away—worried that Eric Schaeffer would . . . Well, when Symbios got your telegram, I knew I'd won."

Tracy stepped back; Marc still held her hands but he made no move to stop her.

"Didn't Elise say you always win?" Her voice was calm, hiding the storm of questions that raged in her mind.

"But never before has so much been at stake. Tracy, I love you, and I want you to be my wife." His eyes were a dark blue, the color of the sky that spread over his land.

OK, Tracy, she said to herself, now you must decide. Is this what you want? Do you want to be the wife of Marc Durand of Brewster, Idaho—a man who constantly keeps you off balance, who makes you feel as if you had caught the tail of a whirlwind and don't dare let go? Well, do you?

"Tracy? I . . ."

She was in Marc's arms so fast that she didn't know who had moved. She answered her own question. Of course she did. Had there ever been any real doubt?

As Marc picked her up Tracy's arms flew around his neck; her kisses covered his face and he laughed at her exuberance.

"Bathtub or bed?"

"On the rooftop in the snow. I don't really care."

"No, thanks. I like my creature comforts," he said, walking into the bedroom.

With fumbling hands and barely suppressed giggles they undressed each other, pausing for long kisses that became a reawakening of their bodies' needs. Soon their combined clothes made an untidy pile on the floor.

Marc started to lay Tracy down on the bed, but she said, "No. I want to look at you first." He stood while Tracy's gaze and hands roamed over his body, touching him intimately as she gloried in the feel of this man she loved.

Finally Marc exhaled raggedly and said, "Tracy, please . . ."

She laughed, a joyous sound that expressed her happiness. Taking his hand, she pulled him onto the bed, quickly wrapping her legs and arms around him as if afraid he'd get away.

With the knowledge born of their previous experiences they aggressively made love to each other, neither one passive or shy or reticent about expressing their pleasure. Marc prepared Tracy for their journey, but just before he took her to the extreme fulfillment he whispered, "Oh, Tracy, I've needed you so badly."

"And what about Symbios?" she murmured.

Marc looked deeply into her eyes. "I want to hire you for both jobs. OK?"

As Tracy welcomed Marc into her being the last thing she remembered saying was, "Oh, yes, Marc . . . yes, yes, yes."

YOU'LL BE SWEPT AWAY
WITH SILHOUETTE DESIRE

$1.75 each

1 ☐ CORPORATE AFFAIR
James

2 ☐ LOVE'S SILVER WEB
Monet

3 ☐ WISE FOLLY
Clay

4 ☐ KISS AND TELL
Carey

5 ☐ WHEN LAST WE LOVED
Baker

6 ☐ A FRENCHMAN'S KISS
Mallory

7 ☐ NOT EVEN FOR LOVE
St. Claire

8 ☐ MAKE NO PROMISES
Dee

9 ☐ MOMENT IN TIME
Simms

10 ☐ WHENEVER I LOVE YOU
Smith

$1.95 each

11 ☐ VELVET TOUCH
James

12 ☐ THE COWBOY AND THE
LADY   Palmer

13 ☐ COME BACK, MY LOVE
Wallace

14 ☐ BLANKET OF STARS
Valley

15 ☐ SWEET BONDAGE
Vernon

16 ☐ DREAM COME TRUE
Major

19 ☐ LOVER IN PURSUIT
James

20 ☐ KING OF DIAMONDS
Allison

21 ☐ LOVE IN THE CHINA SEA
Baker

22 ☐ BITTERSWEET IN BERN
Durant

23 ☐ CONSTANT STRANGER
Sunshine

24 ☐ SHARED MOMENTS
Baxter

25 ☐ RENAISSANCE MAN
James

26 ☐ SEPTEMBER MORNING
Palmer

27 ☐ ON WINGS OF NIGHT
Conrad

28 ☐ PASSIONATE JOURNEY
Lovan

29 ☐ ENCHANTED DESERT
Michelle

30 ☐ PAST FORGETTING
Lind

31 ☐ RECKLESS PASSION
James

32 ☐ YESTERDAY'S DREAMS
Clay

38 ☐ SWEET SERENITY
Douglass

39 ☐ SHADOW OF BETRAYAL
Monet

Silhouette Desire

- 40 ☐ GENTLE CONQUEST Mallory
- 41 ☐ SEDUCTION BY DESIGN St. Claire
- 42 ☐ ASK ME NO SECRETS Stewart
- 43 ☐ A WILD, SWEET MAGIC Simms
- 44 ☐ HEART OVER MIND West
- 45 ☐ EXPERIMENT IN LOVE Clay
- 46 ☐ HER GOLDEN EYES Chance
- 47 ☐ SILVER PROMISES Michelle
- 48 ☐ DREAM OF THE WEST Powers
- 49 ☐ AFFAIR OF HONOR James
- 50 ☐ FRIENDS AND LOVERS Palmer
- 51 ☐ SHADOW OF THE MOUNTAIN Lind
- 52 ☐ EMBERS OF THE SUN Morgan
- 53 ☐ WINTER LADY Joyce
- 54 ☐ IF EVER YOU NEED ME Fulford
- 55 ☐ TO TAME THE HUNTER James
- 56 ☐ FLIP SIDE OF YESTERDAY Douglass
- 57 ☐ NO PLACE FOR A WOMAN Michelle
- 58 ☐ ONE NIGHT'S DECEPTION Mallory
- 59 ☐ TIME STANDS STILL Powers
- 60 ☐ BETWEEN THE LINES Dennis
- 61 ☐ ALL THE NIGHT LONG Simms
- 62 ☐ PASSIONATE SILENCE Monet
- 63 ☐ SHARE YOUR TOMORROWS Dee
- 64 ☐ SONATINA Milan
- 65 ☐ RECKLESS VENTURE Allison
- 66 ☐ THE FIERCE GENTLENESS Langtry

LOOK FOR _A KISS REMEMBERED_ BY ERIN ST. CLAIRE AVAILABLE IN JULY.

Silhouette Desire

Coming Next Month

Gamemaster by Stephanie James

Shelley Banning was an enterprising accountant, but it would take all her skills to outwit Joel Cassidy, the man who engaged her in a passionate love match—one that she was determined to win.

Shadows of Yesterday by Dixie Browning

Chalis Kenyon sought refuge back home at Quarter Moon Pond. But not even the isolated cabin in North Carolina's woods could shelter her from Benjamin Poe and the passions he aroused in her.

Passion's Portrait by Suzanne Carey

The clandestine legacy that Maggie's free-spirited grandmother had left her linked Maggie's family to that of artist Luke Darby. Now Maggie found herself being drawn to Luke and longing for history to repeat itself.

Dinner For Two by Vanessa Victor

As food editor for *Going Places* magazine, Darcy Roberts had often sampled and reviewed exotic dishes in foreign countries but no exotic food she had sampled could ever compare with the enticing Andreas Greogory.

Man Of The House by Janet Joyce

Marcus Stafford was hardly the handyman Lindsey expected. The devastating giant swept Lindsey off her feet. Too quickly he became a fixture in her life, challenging her to abandon the past and build a new future.

Nobody's Baby by Susannah Hart

When Faith was exposed as none other than the hot-blooded novelist Fanny Duvall she knew she'd have to pay, but losing herself in Nick Justin's arms was well worth the cost.